LIT BY LIGHTNING

LIT BY LIGHTNING

A New Orleans Mystery

George Sanchez

"...for nowadays the world is lit by lightning..."—Tennessee Williams,
"The Glass Menagerie"

Southern Girl Press

Cover photo by the author

DEDICATION

Jim and Cindy Robison,
who were there at the start,
and
Jane, Jay, Tasha, Bibbet,
and Miko
Who are the reasons I write

LIT BY LIGHTNING IS FOR

Jim and Cindy Robison,
who were there at the start,
and
Jane, Jay, Tasha, Bibbet,
and Miko
who were there as I wrote

PROLOGUE

NEW ORLEANS is not a place, but a dream, a creation of each and every one touched by her.

Outside, the air was heavy with humidity and the musky smells of the Vieux Carre. The ships (and their crews of horny sailors) that came to unload the produce of the world lay quietly along the docks. The streets were quiet. The daytime mule wagons that carted tourists through the streets to the outrageous lies of the drivers were stabled for the night. Bourbon Street was too far away for the sounds of jazz and vomiting tourists to be heard. The street where the theatre was located was too far off the beaten path to attract traffic. It was a good location for a theatre. It was also a good place to be quiet. I closed my eyes and let the recent past scroll past them.

I was on stage in another theatre, a long way from here, in a much colder city. The play had something to do with a parrot with bad grammar. I can't say I ever understood why that mattered, but they paid me to go on stage and say the lines every night and that is an important thing if the occupation listed on your passport is "actor." How can you prove it if you're not in a play?

Of course, there were drawbacks to the life. Once, I was in a show that called for me to be scruffy and unshaven. I thought I did that very well. Scruffy and unshaven, that is. The critics had varying opinions as to how I had done in the role, but what do they know? The theatre thought well enough of me to pay me regularly. Being scruffy in the mirror was getting depressing, but, hey, I had a regular paycheck for a change so I decided to get some new clothes. I walked into this tony men's store and was browsing for the appropriate threading to cover the body. No salesclerk approached.

Finally, one with a voice like an ice cube came over to grudgingly ask if he could be of assistance. It sounded like the assistance he most wanted to provide was to place his foot sufficiently hard on my butt that I would take my polluting presence out of his low light grandeur. Knowing he was about to metamorphose into a large green toady made me happy so, I listed five or six pieces I had picked out.

---How is this to be paid for, sir?

His voice quavered, but I thought perhaps he was a singer. Everyone in the business needs a straight job, so I paid it no mind.

---Cash, I said, pulling out a wad.

He beamed and, I think, blotted his forehead with a handkerchief. While I was paying, he asked in a strange tone what I did for a living and I told him I was in this play.

He got very chummy after that and confided in a low voice, hie eyes flashing maliciously at the salesclerks who had ignored me.

It seemed the reason I had so much time to browse was that they were all afraid to wait on me. Catching a glimpse of the image I presented, I couldn't blame them. Their honcho finally announced that my scruffy person was driving away customers and something had to be done about me.

He had drawn the short straw and ended up with a decent commission on the sale. I got my clothes and the satisfaction of knowing that I had struck a blow for the underdog. I was doing scruffy very well, indeed.

CHAPTER ONE

The Mississippi River flows past the city of New Orleans in a cocoa swirl of water carrying the richest topsoil in the world down from plains that grow enough food to feed the hungry of all the Third World—were it not for the fact that politicians and corporate fat cats determined years ago that there is more money to be made in not feeding the hungry than in feeding those hungry. The fact that this makes no sense does not bother New Orleans.

As a Mediterranean city, she long ago discarded the notion that life made sense or was fair or moral or just. This doesn't mean that there is no ethos to New Orleans or her children. It simply means that we have our own take on things. Loyalty and family rank a whole lot higher here than in more moral parts of the universe. We have good eyes and long memories, and we take care of our own.

No matter what.

New Orleans is not a place. She is an experience. New Orleans has no star. She is an ensemble piece. I'm sure it's a noble thing to want to see life steadily and whole. You can't do that in New Orleans. It would be too much. Instead, she is served up like tapas—a taste of this, a taste of that. Now you see, and then you don't see. Like a conjuring trick. Or show business. Which I know something about.

Spotlight picks out this player and he has his moment center stage, then it picks out another. On her good days, New Orleans is revealed like the magic lantern show that awed our grandparents in a simpler time or, on bad days, like flashes of lightning in a storm. This part of her is lit and then you lose it. Then another part appears and it's gone. You don't see the whole picture until the storm ends, and the lightning stops.

I was glad to be back. It had been too long. The fact that my exile was self-imposed had nothing to do with it. I would have come back in any event. The coffee and chicory that we brew from Mississippi water that already looks like café au lait long ago replaced whatever flows through my veins, so that my body is subject to the tidal influences that New Orleans imposes on all her children. We are made of Mississippi water and an ethos we imbibe with our mother's milk.

The name "The Big Easy" never made any sense to me. There is nothing easy about life in New Orleans. She is a stern, if loving, mother and her demands on her children are unending. It's not that she imposes a lot of duties or chores like a constant nag. Instead, like the matriarch she is, she demands that we embrace life to the full and become who we were meant to be. That isn't easy, but since it is wrapped in her boundless love for her children, it is palatable. Certainly, it was enough to bring me back. I was here to bathe in the water and honor the family and my baptism began as soon as I got off the bus. I felt the humid air of the city seeping into my body and expelling all of the bad northern water and rigid damyankee thinking through my pores. I was being cleansed even as I claimed my bags. As I started down Tulane Avenue to Elks Place, I looked around at my native soil to see what changes time had wrought.

The years had not been kind to New Orleans. The oil and gas business had gone belly up. The corporations were moving to Texas. The city had emptied into the suburbs, which were fast becoming slums, and AIDS was cutting into the hooker trade. New Orleans really had only one thing to offer on this night, and her bouncing baby boy was back in search of it.

The French Quarter at night has always been a favorite spot for me, as long as the part I'm walking is away from the tourists. I know the tourist commission loves them and the politicians love them and the shop owners love them, but I don't. In the city I knew, the French Quarter was just another neighborhood, and neighborhoods are what New Orleans is all about. You could go to a different part of town and be in a totally different place. You never had to see the world, if you grew up in New Orleans, it was already here. Except for mountains. I like mountains.

So, I ambled down streets where people actually lived and passed stores where they shopped for the basics, and bars where there were no exotic drinks. And I never heard a hard Midwestern "r" spoken. I was happy. The tourist commission would not approve, but the only person I knew on the tourist commission had retired so I wasn't worried about offending anyone.

My grousing had brought me where I was going, so I stopped outside a brick wall that had grass and flowers growing on top between the broken bottle glass. I looked up at the wooden sign. *Cirque de Theatre.* I was there.

There was no one in the patio or box office. The lobby was heavy with the smell of stale cigarette smoke and littered with sandwich papers and soft drink bottles, so no show was on. All I'd be disturbing was rehearsal, and I had a standing invitation to walk into one of those whenever I wanted. I stood for a few minutes letting my eyes adjust to the dim rehearsal lighting, and then slid into a seat on the back row. The first one was loose and rocked under me, which was not a surprise, I remembered the place well, so I found another.

It looked like the rehearsal was good for another thirty minutes, at least, so I slid deeper into the seat and let my eyes wander around the darkness of the theatre. It hadn't changed much in the years since I left. There were two tiers with two rows each on either side of the bleachers where I was sitting. The whole place was painted black and the lights hung about twelve feet above the rectangle of the tile-floored stage. The set was under construction against the fourth wall. I couldn't make out what it would be yet.

It had been my home before I left. I hadn't gone looking for the bright lights of Broadway. I just wanted to practice my chosen trade. Well, my second chosen trade. The first one had been a mistake, on my part and on the part of those who hired me. I didn't think I had retreated into acting, even if I had pulled it over my head like a flannel blanket to hide from the dark. I had just moved on from a vocation I didn't fit, and was trying on a different persona with every role I played.

I slid down on my spine and rested my head against the edge of the seat back. Don was hunkered in the front row. His long arms dangled between his equally long legs and were capped by two huge hands. One of them held a cigarette between two orange fingers. An ashtray directly underneath caught the ash as it fell from the glowing end. Judging from the number of butts, things had not been going well. I could wait.

Outside, the air was heavy with humidity and the musky smells of the Vieux Carre. The ships (and their crews of horny sailors) that came to unload the produce of the world lay quietly along the docks. The streets were quiet. The daytime mule wagons that carted tourists through the streets to the outrageous lies of the drivers were stabled for the night. Bourbon Street was too far away for the sounds of jazz and vomiting tourists to be heard. The street where the theatre was located was too far off the beaten path to attract traffic. It was a good location for a theatre. It was also a good place to be quiet. I closed my eyes and let the recent past scroll behind them.

I needed a little clarification. Backstage at my Midwest Theatre gig, I had received a telegram saying, "Father found dead. Come home soonest."

That someone dies, you come to expect. The wording of the telegram, particularly "found dead," was different. It had a question dangling from it like the worst participle you ever saw.

The bus ride had taken eighteen hours. Flying would have been faster, but the bus provides time to think; time to appreciate the country you are traveling through; and time to interact with your fellow passengers. Besides, I was afraid of airplanes.

So, I headed home. There were people to see. There might be action to take, but that could wait. I'd start by paying visits to old friends and acquaintances. A talk with my best friend was my reason for sitting in a theatre in the dark.

I opened my eyes when I heard a voice. A short blonde with carved features repeated her question.

---Who, or what, are you?

That was a fairly existential question so, rather than answer it right away, I decided to spend my time getting a good look at her. She was worth a second look, and probably a third, fourth, and fifth as well. I shouldn't be taking all that time looking. There was serious business to conduct, but what is life if you don't indulge yourself?

She was wearing a sleeveless pink tee shirt cut off above the navel. A quick look established that her navel was an "innie." Her skin was very fair. Her short blonde hair was tucked into a newsboy cap that shadowed her eyes. Worn jeans with a lot of paint on them covered a nice span of hips—not huge, but very well proportioned.

I thought I was being as surreptitious as hell. Covert looks were a specialty of mine. Not that I was spying. I knew when I was spying and I wasn't spying. At least, I didn't think I was. She made me wonder.

---Finished? she asked.

---Only with a first look, I said.

--That's all you'll ever get.

--This is no way to start a relationship, I said.

--But a perfect way to end one, she snorted.

--Your life is your own, but I wouldn't piss her off, if I were you, said a familiar bass voice.

I looked up. Don was grinning over her shoulder.

--Hard ass? I asked.

--Stage manager, he replied.

---Take my head off, would she?

---Ever seen a good stage manager who couldn't? he asked.

---Not one of yours.

I had forgotten the stage manager, which was one of the stupidest things I'd ever done. Maybe that offended her.

---Would you two like to be alone? she asked.

---Only if you promise to come back, I said, ---I require further knowledge of you.

---Carnal knowledge? That you can forget, she said. ---For any other kind, try the library.

She walked away and I wondered if she always moved like that or if there was a particular swing to her hips that was just for me. She did a slight pause and a half glance over her shoulder. It was for me and I felt very happy. I was right about her butt. It was perfectly proportioned for her build, and sufficiently rounded to disturb my sleep for weeks.

---I think I'm in love, I said.

---I've never known you not to be, Don answered. ---I need to grab a cigarette.

The small patio was cool for a New Orleans summer night. The fronds of the elephant ear plants and the water that trickled down the wall to fill the lily pond probably helped. I hooked a wrought iron bench with my foot and plunked into it hiking my feet on the pond's edge. Don lit one of the far too many cigarettes he smoked and leaned against the palm. Cigarette in the corner of his mouth and smoke dribbling from his nose, he took a long look at me before he inhaled.

---Well? he asked.

The red lanterns overhead combined with the green light shining up under the plants to color his face like a Hindu painting. It was so blatantly obvious, I felt compelled to point it out.

---You look like a Hindu painting, I said.

---Not a Buddha, I trust, he grunted.

He was six foot three and weighed about one hundred and fifty.

---Not unless there's famine, I said.

---Tell me what brings you home. I'm having trouble with the scene and I have to get back.

---You still have a bed open for me?

It may seem that I was shattering the bonds of polite society with my terseness, but he wouldn't think so. We were friends. Besides, he was from Michigan, and those people know nothing about Southern gentility.

---Here's the key. I'll be home in about two hours.

---Two hours? You really are having trouble with the scene. Why?

---When I get home, I'll tell you my sad story and you can tell me yours.

---Deal, I said.

He dropped his cigarette butt in a planter and went back into the theatre. I decided to get another look at the stage manager before I left. I wanted something from her. Well, I wanted a lot from her, but her name would do for a start.

She wasn't in the seating area so I drifted backstage. She was squatting in the alley that ran alongside the theatre, painting a row of flowers on a flat. I am very grateful that she had to squat because it confirmed my suspicion about her behind. It was a relief to know that my powers of deduction were still keen. If *that* goes, all that's left is musical comedy.

---You're in my light.

---Sorry. Is this the way to the men's room?

--- You know damn well where the men's room is. You've done enough shows here, Chaussier.

---You asked about me? I'm touched.

---I dust the lobby once a week. Your pictures are on the wall. They're kind of faded. You must be very old.

---If you want to insult me, why not just say ugly things about my mama?

---I might like your mama.

---Why you think that?

---I like people who have known suffering. If she brought you into the world, she's suffered.

---Besides insulting wealthy benefactors to the theatre, what do you do around here?

---Everything. And if you're a wealthy benefactor, I'll kiss your butt.

---*There's* a thought that could inspire me to make a lot of money fast.

She stopped painting for a minute and I might have seen a little reddening to her cheeks. It was hard to be sure. Her face was in shadow. Come to think of it, I had never had a good look at her face. Maybe she heard the thought, because she turned to me and the light caught her squarely.

It had been a long trip. That's probably why my heart stopped. On the other hand, maybe she was as much of a knockout as I thought.

You've heard the expression, "sculptured features?" That's what she had in a Greta Garbo, Ingrid Bergman kind of way. Her eyes weren't Scandinavian, though. They had a slight slant to them and they looked gold in the light. What she was doing backstage when she belonged in One (that's the star spot center stage) if anyone ever did, I couldn't imagine. Certainly, she could play a leading role in my life. I was probably staring. I know I came to when she spoke.

---You're a friend of Don's.

---An old friend.

-- A very old friend.

---Another cut to the heart. I'll leave before you get really vicious.

---Good plan.

---I'm going, but I'll be back.

---Thanks for the warning.

I gave her a gracious bow and headed into the theatre.

---Bryna, she said.

---What?

---My name. If that's why you're interrupting my work.

---That was part of it.

---What was the rest?

---I wanted to sneak a look at your butt.

Was there that reddening again as she turned back to her painting? A blushing stage manager would be something entirely new in my experience.

---My name is Jeff...

---I know your name, Chaussier, she said.

---How long will it take to get on a first name basis with you?

She eyed me critically for what I felt to be much too long a time. About the time I started to wonder if I had reached the stage of plastic surgery, she finally answered.

---Not tonight.

I decided that was a hopeful statement and I had better close on it. The French Quarter seemed like a very nice place on the walk to Don's apartment.

The night had cooled a little, or, at least, the fog off the river made it seem cool. It wasn't a truly foggy night, but there was enough in the air to make little haloes around the streetlights. Tourist revels on Bourbon Street sounded far away and the foot traffic was light. It seemed peaceful. It was so peaceful, in fact, that it was fairly easy to pick up the sounds of footsteps following me.

Now, I'm not so paranoid that I think people are out to get me. At least, not all the time. So, when I thought I picked up the sound, I used a darkened plate glass window in a closed grocery store to check for other pedestrians. I didn't see anyone. I walked at an easy pace, stopping to look at creole cottages as if I had never seen one before and, sure enough, there was someone there.

I had my duffel bag across my back and I stopped to shift it and, just a little too slow to escape my eagle eye, I saw a figure duck between two cars about a block away. Now, it's possible he was picking up cans to sell for scrap. It's possible he was a bashful fan of my work. There are a lot of possibilities in the world, and I like to sort them out. Call it a hobby.

With elaborate ease, I stretched my head, examining the lacy wrought iron balconies overhead. I had small interest in wrought iron balconies, but it gave me a reason to casually stroll back in his direction, oh-so-unaware of his presence. I managed to get within a few car lengths of him and, just when I was running through my repertoire of opening remarks which range from, "Hi, sailor, new in town?" to "Why the hell are you following me?" he sprinted across the street and down the block. I thought I saw him climb into a big-ass black sedan, but it was so dark, it might have been a red Mustang.

It's possible, he remembered a pressing engagement. It's possible I needed to change colognes. I thought it was more likely that my nasty suspicious mind had just scored a goal. Somebody in town was interested in my movements. I wondered how many people knew I was in town. I wondered who needed to know I was in town and why.

I walked on, although at a slow pace, with a lot of rubbernecking and my ears strained so much that they were pointy by the time I got to Don's.

CHAPTER TWO

The stairs were as narrow as I remembered and the white wall to the right still had dust layered on the mortar between the bricks. The wood supports were that dark color that said the building had been there for a long time. It was probably an old carriage house. Don liked to call it slave quarters when he was trying to get a raise from the board of directors, but I doubted it was.

The neon light from the restaurant on the corner spilled through the window high overhead and the banana tree in the patio cast colored shadows on the steps. I stopped for a look. The lush green patio was the reason Don kept the apartment in the first place.

I moved carefully up the stairs. There was no railing and as my eyes reached floor level, they were met by two brown eyes and bared teeth. A large dog barred my path with a low growl in his throat. His feet were planted and he reared back ready to tear me apart. At least, he would have if I had been an eighty-year-old woman or a four-year-old girl.

---Hello, Marc, I said. He licked my face. I always hated that.

Marc, (full name either Marc Antony or Marcus Aurelius, it varied) was a pure-bred basset hound with beautiful tricolor markings. When Marc came to live with Don, (it would be inappropriate to say Don bought him, or, heaven forbid, owned him) he had been named by the breeder. Don tried to change it to Marcus Aurelius, but the dog would only react to his own proper name.

Marc Antony greeted me at the head of the stairs. If he knew you, you were home free. As I had bunked many times with Don for a variety of familial and economic reasons, I was greeted as one of the family. Which put my life in danger. Bassets are not teacup dogs.

Trying not to trip over him as he snaked through my legs, I mounted the last few steps to the apartment. Well, really, it was one large room with an open kitchen at one end. There was a bedroom in the far wall and a bathroom off that. Other than that, it was open space with brick walls, wood beams, high ceilings and enough ambiance to make the tourist commission bust a gut out of sheer civic pride. Maybe the Quarter did look like they claimed it did.

There was the usual clutter of art around, much of it obviously local. Don liked to support people he knew by buying their work, but to describe it all would take a catalogue. There was a real beauty over the couch. It was a portrait of a young man, but the colors were vivid and intense. Bright colors picked out the highlights and there were shades of blue for the shadows of the face. It made him seem a good deal more interesting than he probably was. I don't know enough about art to characterize the style. It wasn't realistic, nor was it surreal. It was an apparently exact portrait executed in what, to me, was an unconventional style that told me a lot about the subject and made me wonder about the artist.

The Modigliani and Picasso prints were in their customary places. Other than that, there were a couple of small Quarter-inspired pieces--paintings of wrought iron from so close that, if you didn't know what they were, you would have thought that you were looking at abstractions. I saw no new sculpture, but the abstract iron angel and the Easter Island head carved from a piece of nice redwood always pleased me. There was a very fine head of a rugged, but clean-featured man, Carthaginian, I'd been told. It was only about two or three inches high, but it represented the man so well that I felt I knew his life story.

My yawn reminded me I was tired. It had been a long trip and a tension-filled few days. I couldn't go to sleep yet. I needed to talk to Don when he got in. Besides, Marc was a night owl and if I tried to stake out the couch too early, I would have paws up my nose. As long as I sat up, he didn't care, so I decided to have a drink, pretend to watch television, and catch a few winks without disturbing Marc, who was extremely territorial for a basset hound.

Turning on the television, I went through the arch that defined the kitchen area and got ice. Then I took the bottle of Cutty Sark and poured a glassful. Stretching my legs on the magazine-covered coffee table, I leaned my head back against the couch and closed my eyes to think.

Maybe this was a fool's errand. There were no grounds to suppose that anything other than an accident caused my father's death. There were no known quarrels in his life; he didn't owe money; he had no obvious enemies. There had been a police investigation, because all deaths that occur away from a doctor's care are investigated.

This deserved careful consideration and I decided to devote the next two hours to thinking about it.

Don kicked my feet off the table and I woke to a glass full of ice water with a yellow layer on the bottom where the scotch had settled.

---You're disturbing my dog, he said.

---I am not. He's watching television with me.

---Marc hates police shows. He thinks they lack character development.

---You're making that up.

---Ask him.

---What do you think of the show, Marc?

Basset flatulence filled the air.

---Told you.

---He does that all the time anyway.

---Want a drink?

---Got one.

---You have a glass of faintly colored water. Do you want a drink?

---Is it macrobiotic? I'm trying to live healthy.

---Organically made by little people living on the shores of Loch Ness according to a Druid recipe engraved on the wall of a nearby cave.

---With that much history, it would be rude not to.

He poured a water glass three quarters full of water, added ice and a dash of scotch. That was for me. He didn't use ice cubes. He said the refraction of the light through the ice was aesthetically unpleasing. Personally, I think he didn't want to sacrifice that much room in the glass.

He sat in the red canvas bucket chair across from me. First, he took a long pull on his glass, then he let a lot of air escape his lungs in a protracted sigh, finally, he lit a cigarette. That meant he was home and conversation could begin.

---Boudreaux, he said.

---Boudreaux ?

---You didn't get her last name.

---Did she tell you to give it to me?

---In your dreams.

---How'd you know I didn't know her last name?

---Instinct.

---How'd you know I wanted it?

---Experience.

Bryna Boudreaux. Alliterative as all hell. Don't ask if I thought it fit her. I am completely incompetent on certain subjects. It's like asking me someone's age. I always assume the person I'm speaking to is as old as I am. Sometimes, maybe, more wrinkled.

Perhaps I should ask her out and get to know her as a way of expanding my knowledge of my fellow man. Or woman. There was much I could get to know about her. For starters, I should know if she were straight or gay—always a good question in the theatre—or androgynous, married, committed, or available. What this had to do with my visit I did not know. It certainly seemed a subject worth exploring. But, sitting there salivating over the help wasn't good guest behavior, so I decided to ask Don about the show first.

---What trouble are you having with the show?

---Besides incompetence, ignorance, illegitimacy, tertiary syphilis, and the wrong end of the gene pool?

---Besides those.

---Putting those aside, it's going fine.

---Glad to hear it.

---What are you back for?

---My father.

---I know about your father. He's already buried. You could

have sent flowers, put in a lachrymose phone call to your mother, and that would have been acceptable. Instead, you're here. Why?

---I'm wondering if his death needs explaining.

---To who? The police seem all right with the accident theory. Why not you?

I took a sip of the scotch. I used to love the stuff. I seldom drank now. Perhaps because I loved the stuff too well. Don waited across the room, his face and his glass roughly on the same level as his knees as he sat sunk in the chair. He was in no hurry for an answer so I took my time in coming up with one.

---He had no intention of dying.

---Few of us do, but we end up doing it anyway.

---And if that's how it turns out, I'm OK with it. I just want the circumstances of his death very clear in my mind with absolutely no little whispers in the back of my head.

---Is there anything that would put those whispers in your head?

---Yes.

---Ah.

There followed some smoking and drinking on his part and a lot of staring into a nearly full glass on my part.

---None of my business, he finally said into the silence, ---but I seem to recall that you didn't always get along well with your father.

---And so?

---Why this—investigation? he asked.

That called for a long drink and a short pause. Lying to him would be worse than useless, but there was no way I could tell him the truth, so I came up with the best reason I could.

---Immanuel Kant, I said.

---Now you're being cryptic.

---The categorical imperative.

---Ah, he said.

There are things that you simply have to do. No matter what, when, where, or why. You simply have to do them. He knew that as well as I did. This was one.

17

He did some more smoking and drinking and I did my staring into the glass trick and time passed. I may have dozed. I do know that Don stood up and patted his thigh.

---Here, Marc.

---What's up?

---I'm going to take him out for his walk. Stretch out. You look like hell. I'll lock Marc in the room with me tonight so you can get a decent rest. You look like you need it.

---Thanks.

He got the metal link leash and headed down the steps with Marc noisily preceding him, claws scrabbling on the stairs. Just as his head was about to disappear down the stairwell, Don stopped.

---Like the picture over the couch?

---Love it. Why?

---She painted it.

---She? Who?

He snorted and continued down the steps without answering. I stretched out to look at the painting. I had known from the first that I wanted to know the artist. Now that I knew who painted it, it became a matter of some urgency.

Why do a portrait with colors that vivid and intense? The bright colors picking out the highlights and the blues deepening the shadows of the face that caught my attention now reminded me of my too brief glimpse of Bryna. She was like that, bold direct and strong, but the eyes suggested a level of mystery and a degree of pain. Is that a lot to read from a quick meeting in dim theatre light?

I started thinking about her a little too much for a man who might yet spend the night with a basset hound and I didn't think Don would take kindly to my disgracing myself with his dog, so I turned to other topics. Like what I was here for.

My mind played in a lazy way with things I had been told about how my father occupied his days since retiring from the fire department. He was never going to be comfortable sitting in a rocking chair, but he started keeping some strange hours. My father was an interesting man. Maybe my mother understood him. I can't say I did. Admired? Respected? Loved? Yes. Understood? No. I never knew what made him tick. I asked him about it once and he just looked incredibly wise.

---You're an actor. You're good at discovering motivations, he had said. ---Treat me like a part you're playing.

That might not be bad advice in the current situation. It was a process I knew well. I told myself that tomorrow I'd start on the cast of characters, which started me thinking about plays and theatre which started me thinking about an alliterative name. And the face that went with it.

I rested my eyes for just a minute and suddenly there was that face with the clean features of a Greta Garbo except for the slight slant to eyes that had a glint of gold that cut right to where you lived when they looked at you with that firm direct stare. I think I smiled. At least Don said I was smiling when he pulled a cover over me before taking Marc into the bedroom.

I hate people who talk about their dreams. Let me tell you my dream.

I was on stage in a play and I didn't know the name of it or what my role was or my next line and all the other actors were looking at me as if it was my cue. If you're waiting for the part where I'm naked, forget it. It wasn't that dream. Though, like every actor who ever lived, I've had that dream more than once.

The faces of the other actors were hidden, but the faces in the audience were clear. I saw my brothers and my mother and my uncle and a bunch of other people that I had known growing up. They were waiting for me. I didn't know if they were waiting for me to say the line I didn't know or if they were waiting for me to bow or what. When I looked back at the stage one of the actors turned to me and I knew those slanted golden eyes. I kept wishing she would turn so I could see her butt, then I remembered again it wasn't that kind of dream.

I tried to ask her what line I was supposed to say, but just when I opened my mouth to speak, a shadow from behind me fell across her face and she looked frightened. I turned to tell the guy to bug off but all I could see was that huge shadow. Then, I swear, I heard my father's voice coming from below the stage like the Ghost in

"Hamlet." He was saying something but I couldn't make out the words because the levee must have broken. I heard a roar and a great flood of *café au lait* Mississippi River water gushed onto the stage. Then Bryna screamed. I turned to her voice. The big shadow was trying to drown her. Only her face was above water and his hand was atop her head pushing down.

The rising water kept me from getting to her but, just as she was about to go under, a huge axe swung down to cut off the hand pushing on her head and she bobbed up. I didn't try to sneak a peek, even if she was nude. I wanted to. After all, I'm human. The voice below the stage called again and I turned to look, but no one was there except my mother who was stirring a cup of tea and looking at me with eyes that told me there was something I had to do and I had better do it.

Then I woke up. I didn't know what any of that meant. Fantasy or prologue, I knew why my father and my family were there. Bryna's presence was harder to explain. Even if she was nude for a flash.

CHAPTER THREE

With all the soft surfaces, in the entire apartment, Marc had to choose his customary couch to sleep on. That may not be a thought of blinding clarity, but you wake up with a basset butt in your face and see how eloquent you are. The door to Don's bedroom was ajar. I suppose Marc had pushed it open to press his territorial claim to the couch.

It was a little before noon. I knew Don wouldn't be up for an hour yet, so I gave Marc a dog biscuit, threw water on my face, and headed out the door. I didn't need to dress, because I had never undressed. I needed to... husband... my wardrobe (I love words.) Anyway, I hadn't brought much.

I stopped at a diner where the waiters were rude and the place dirty, but they served breakfast any time of the day or night, and they served a lot of it. For gracious, expensive dining, see the tourist bureau. I was hungry.

As I did my second cup of coffee, I tried to decide where to go first. I had a lot of catching up to do. Since nothing was clicking, I decided not to rush the coffee. It was nice to be back in a place where you couldn't see the bottom of the cup through the brew. Even without the chicory, New Orleans coffee put hair on your chest. What it did for women, I didn't want to think about, but that did get me to thoughts of the female sex.

Principally of the stage manager who may well have been at the theatre working. I didn't want to seem too eager, so I decided not to go. I hated myself for deciding not to go, but I didn't. Character is important. Instead I went through the Quarter and caught the bus to City Park. I wasn't a nature lover; I wanted to see a man about a man.

I went in the back way, opened the latch on the rusted gate, and took the few steps up the concrete sidewalk to the garage door with the chipped white paint.

I opened the door within a door and let my eyes adjust to the dim light inside. The pool table was heaped with clean clothing, computer parts, and magazines. As usual. The work light was on over a workbench strewn with computer parts, pieces of bicycles, guitars, and works in progress. As usual. Bent over a tiny circuit board with his glasses on his forehead and a jeweler's loupe in his eye was Space.

His bald head was pointed directly at me as he shifted the piece around trying to catch the light from the long narrow windows in the garage door.

---Hand me that tube of glue, he said.

I looked on the workbench and didn't see a tube of glue, but then, I couldn't have found an elephant in all the clutter. His hand pawed in the air and pointed behind me.

---On the pool table, he said.

This was even more hopeless, because a T-Rex could have hidden there and I wouldn't have found him.

---Pick up the Popular Mechanics, look to the right of the National Geographic, and under the Tulane sweatshirt.

The damn thing was right there, of course. He knew where everything in the house was. Clutter never bothered him. It wasn't clutter to him; it was just his own peculiar system of organization.

He fiddled for a few seconds with something too tiny to be seen with anything less than an electron microscope, then blew out his breath in a slow, hissing sigh.

---Got you, he said.

I waited as patiently as I could. If it had been anyone else, I might have been angry, but that would have been a complete and utter waste of time with Space. He was what he was, and he worked the way he worked, and the only reason for putting up with his eccentricities was that he was good at everything he did. If he ever found a thing he wasn't good at, he worked at it with the patience of Ariadne at her web until he was.

---Anything else I can do for you? I asked.

---Yes, he said, ---you can kiss me hello on the top of my greasy, bald head, get me a beer from the fridge and pull us up a couple of chairs on the patio.

---Kiss your own head. I'll meet you outside.

He laughed his patented silent laugh without looking up as he finished whatever it was he was doing. I got a beer for him out of the fridge by the washer/dryer, took two steps, kissed the top of his head, and ducked out the side door.

---I knew you couldn't resist me, he said.

The patio was the side alley to the house where he had rigged an awning over a couple of folding chairs. He had a sand bucket for an ash tray and a stool for his feet. There were plants stuck in old coffee cans on the side stairs and down the alley. Every one of them was green and lush and healthy. I don't think he did anything special to get them that way. I think they just grew on their own, because they knew that, if they didn't, he would get out his tool kit and fiddle with them until they did.

I may have admired him more than anyone I knew because he was so—I don't know—effortless. Not that his life had been easy. It hadn't. He suffered the same woes and pains that all of us do, but it never became a flag that he hung out to say, "pity me, pity me." He just proceeded with the business of living life. He was wonderful with his hands. He was creative. I don't know how many musical instruments he played. I don't know how many pictures he painted. I'll bet, if I could search his place, I would uncover a treasure trove of things anyone else would kill to have created. It didn't seem to matter to him. He took divorce, and losing the use of his legs by falling off a ladder, as he took the ability to create. Just part of life. Most of all, I loved to look into his eyes. They were the warmest eyes I had ever known, and the wisest. When I looked into his eyes, I knew that it was going to be all right. Whatever "it" was. He was more our father than any of us, which was why he was the first person I went to see as my journey began.

He came out the side door drying his hands on a kitchen towel, took the beer off the stool, hopped as he sat down, set his crutches to the side, grunted as he lifted his feet up, one leg at a time, took a hit on his beer and said, ---Where you been?

I hadn't seen him for two years. If it had been twenty, he would have asked the same thing in the same tone. The phlegmatic air with which he worked on anything mechanical was the same air with which he approached life. God, I envied him that quality.

The fact that I had stepped into theatre light to earn a living was a source of scorn on the part of some of my family. That was OK. You don't have to understand me to love me. If you could do both, that was a pearl beyond price. That was what I found in Space. I had always hoped to find it in a girl with whom I could nest and build a life that made sense. That hadn't worked out. The fact that I was searching for this person among actresses may have been a factor in my failure. They are lovely women, but perhaps more touched with the bacchantes than is good for any relationship.

---Here and there.

---Acting?

---Among other things.

He gave the silent laugh that I knew so well and took a pull on his beer. He leaned back in the chair and, from the way the light hit him, he looked more like my father than ever.

---Seen Mom?

---Not yet.

That was a scene I preferred to defer as long as I could. There would be too much pain in the meeting. There would be love, but there would be hurt. I had the idea that, if I could go to her with a neat little package that, somehow, made sense of what had happened, the grief would become a rite of healing. Eventually you had to face the pain, like you had to face the dark inside each one of us, if there was ever to be hope of getting back into the light. That was a process I knew something about.

---When?

Space's question brought me back to the alleyway. I thought for a bit.

---When I know.

He nodded his head like that was a full answer, and maybe it was. Then, he looked off into the distance.

---You know anything? I asked.

He shook his head slowly from side to side.

---You got any questions?

He nodded his head up and down.

---Done anything about it yet?

---Waiting for you.

---Now I'm here.

---You're here.

He took another long pull on his bottle and looked at me from the side of his eye. I knew that he was looking at my untouched beer. I knew he would. He didn't say anything. He wouldn't. He had been with me through a bad time and was as responsible as anyone for the fact that I came out on the other side. He could look all he wanted. He'd never ask. I knew that, but I also knew that he would be there if I needed him again.

---When was the last time you saw him...before? I asked.

---About a week.

---And?

---Something in his craw. You know what he'uz like when he got mad?

---Yeah. I remember him mad.

---He was mad.

---At who?

---It was more of a "something" than a "who," if you know what I mean, but he was going to do something about it.

He took another pull on his beer and this time I joined him. Well, I wet my lips on the bottle. I didn't drink much anymore because I had found that it was seldom a good idea. I found that by drinking more than my share after a particularly bad time in my life and decided that maybe beer was contra-indicated as a regular beverage. I looked over at Space. He was sipping slowly. I never saw him drink fast. I seldom saw him drink a lot. He drank like he did most things---slowly, surely, and very, very efficiently.

---You still got my stuff stored? I asked.

---You need it?

---Not yet.

---It's here.

I wet my lips with the beer and rolled the bottle across my forehead. The cool wetness felt good on what was already a hot day. Summer in New Orleans is not for sissies, but then, New

Orleans is not for sissies. Forget that Big Easy stuff, I tell you. Yeah, the good times roll and the people are more laid back than anywhere else in the United States, but that's because we know what life is really like. And we face it.

---Where should I start? I asked.

---Try Unc.

---Then?

---You know.

He didn't say anything more than that, but he didn't have to. All of us possessed a kind of telepathy that allowed us to communicate anywhere, at any time, and no one ever knew we were communicating at all. I suppose it was spooky. I know it was comforting. I stood up to go.

Perspiration beaded on the top of his head. He looked at me from under his eyebrows. My father's eyes, brown, warm and infinitely wise, looked up at me.

---What you gonna do? he asked.

---Whatever it is, you'll know.

---If it turns out that you have to, make it right.

---By any means necessary.

I walked down the chain link fence to the gate at the end.

---Might be an idea to get that stuff of mine out of storage.

---Already did.

---It's here?

---When you want it.

I hoped I wouldn't need it. I didn't want it near me, because I was afraid I might want to use it. On anybody who happened to be around.

A long time ago, I had begun training to do something. I didn't last very long. I had signed on because I am, by nature, a true believer. In any damn fool thing or person who comes along. I did not like to remember the things I would have been called on to do, because just thinking about it led to nightmares, and I watered those horses with more alcohol than was good for them. Or me. It wasn't that the recruiter had lied about what I would be doing, though he had. It wasn't that I didn't think I could do what the training called for. It was that I knew, without a shadow of a doubt, that I would like doing it far too much and that wouldn't be a good thing.

Space had been there for me when I decided to transition from my nightmare world to a pleasant world of my own devising. It had to be Space because anyone else would have judged me or offered advice or talked at me "for my own good." Space didn't. He just took his huge heart and wrapped me in it until I was ready to step out into the light. Even if it was the pink light of the stage. There, I could show the things I had found in myself in a setting that would not get me arrested or condemned as the moral failure I knew I would have become.

---I love you, brother. I said.

---Back at you.

He brought the beer bottle to his eyebrow in a salute. I gave him the James Dean slide of my hand. The corners of his mouth twitched, but he didn't smile. The eyes looking back at me were far too sober for that.

CHAPTER FOUR

It was hot on the plaza. The heat radiated off the white of the Civil Courts Building, reflected off the glass panels of the library, and zeroed in on me as I approached the green structure which announced across the top, in case you didn't know, "City Hall." I was glad to have that cleared up.

I stopped to look at the building and got the creepy crawlies up my back again. I turned to see who was damn fool enough to stand on the plaza in that heat in order to stare at me. I couldn't be sure. Beneath a tree, a guy was sitting on a bench fanning his shiny face with a newspaper. Another guy had stopped with his foot propped on one of the big planters to tie his shoelace. Under the overhang of the building a woman nuzzled a cigarette, blowing out the smoke in angry puffs. A taxpayer, I thought.

None of them was wearing a London Fog trench coat. Nobody had a sweeping black mustache. Well, maybe the woman. And, although all three of them wore sunglasses, none of them was speaking up a sleeve into a microphone.

I put my reaction off to incipient paranoia—although it's not paranoia if they really are out to get you. Having this feeling twice in two days was enough to force me into a resolution—if anyone was following me I would take action; if there was no one following me, I would get help. Maybe from the stage manager. If she was willing to give me the kind of help I wanted from her. But I was hot enough standing on the plaza and I didn't need the additional heat her image added, so I went inside. It was a lot cooler. As I opened the glass door, I thought I saw the reflection of a big black car passing, but, hey, there must be a lot of black cars in New Orleans.

The seal of the city in the terrazzo floor of the lobby looked the same as ever. I headed for the bank of elevators and hit the button for the sixth floor, trying not to hear the two people in there with me as they discussed an obvious bribe they planned to offer the recorder of mortgages. Times certainly had changed. At one time, they could have bought him for a whole lot less.

In his corner office, tilted back in his chair, and surrounded by more green objects than seemed healthy in a sub-tropical climate, Unc was on the phone. His curly, black hair had more sprinkles of gray than I recalled, and the jaw line under his tanned skin was a little softer than I remembered. On the other hand, his athlete's build under the gray silk suit looked good and his eyes still snapped like bullets as he gave the unfortunate on the other end of the line what for.

He had been in office for a long time, it seemed. It was hard to tell how long, because his father had held the office before him. It was not a matter of nepotism; it was a matter of delivering the goods to the people you represent. I could remember him getting phone calls at his kitchen table, at wedding receptions, at funerals, probably when he was in the bathtub, though I'd never seen him. Somebody would call with a hard luck story, and he would listen patiently, even when the story dragged on forever, then promise to look into it, hang up, make another call, and life would get better for whoever called him.

He wasn't a blood relative. What bound us together was something deeper than that. I respected him. A lot of people respected him. Which was why he kept getting elected. He never took election for granted. Even if the opponent seemed to be a patsy or somebody who put his name up hoping to get bought off to drop out of the race, he always campaigned hard. I asked him why one time and he said that it was only polite to ask for somebody's vote. The people who voted for him liked to be asked and they liked the fact that he always did.

The phone conversation was one of the lengthy ones. He swiveled in his chair, saw me, and waved me in. He was still talking so I checked out the Irish paraphernalia that accounted for the greenish tint of the light. I saw shamrocks and shillelaghs and maps and mugs and beads and glasses and hand embroidered prayers to St. Patrick and Irish drinking toasts. Just when I was ready to fly to England to spit on the Union Jack, he got off the phone.

---Long time.

---Yep.

---I don't have to ask what brought you back.

---Nope.

---You came here with a big scorecard that you intend to check off.

---Would I do that?

---O'course not, he smiled.

---Have you told anyone I was coming?

---People who don't know you don't need to be told.

---What about people who do know me?

He looked up from under those brows that could lower over his eyes like a curtain being drawn to end a scene.

---They don't need to be told either, do they?

I let that sit there a moment.

---Was he into anything? Anything dangerous? Anything he shouldn't have been into?

---I would never be so foolish as to tell your father there was something that was none of his business.

---'Course not.

---I did worry about him. Something was up.

---What?

---He wouldn't say. I couldn't ask.

God, I loved his generation. They were people who grew up with a sterner code than we did. The fact that it was unspoken made it all the stronger. If Kant hadn't done it first, these were the people who would have invented the categorical imperative.

---You're planning on playing Sherlock, aren't you? he asked.

---Maybe.

---I'm not going to tell you not to. It'd be a waste of time and breath. Besides, I don't want to. Somebody's gotta look into it. You as good a candidate as any.

---Maybe better, I said softly.

The sharp brown eyes under the heavy black brows glinted. He rubbed a brown hand across a blue jaw that always seemed to need a shave and looked at me for what seemed like a long time. But, when he spoke, I knew a decision had been reached.

---Where do I fit in? he asked.

I thought about it. I could only say so much, but he knew that, like he knew I wouldn't say anything that he might have to testify to on a Bible. Circumlocution is a fine thing in many situations.

---Get me some maneuvering room?

He thought before answering. I think he always did, even at the times when his answer came fast. In politics, you don't say what you can nod, don't nod what you can smile, don't smile what you can wink, so I was a little surprised when he chose the retort direct.

---I can get you some cooperation. I can get you a little slack. I can't get you out of a murder rap.

---It won't come to that.

---I hope not.

There was just a hint in his voice that was a statement of boundaries. He would help as much as he could, but he wouldn't break the law. He had a very good sense of balance and he was telling me that if I started out on the tightrope under the circus lights, I had better be carrying an umbrella, because there was no net below.

---How's your mother?

Ah, I knew that one was coming. I tried to deflect the question with one of my own.

---You haven't seen her?

---Not since the funeral.

---If I find out, I'll let you know.

---You haven't been to see your mother?

I gave him an answer he would understand.

---Don't want her to know anything she might have to swear to on a Bible.

He nodded. I stood to leave.

---Tell Aunt Marie hello for me.

His voice was uninflected, but I knew he was telling me something.

---Don't want her at risk any more than you want your mother at risk.

We let all the spoken and unspoken content of our conversation hang in the air for a moment while we weighed it against how much we wanted to put on the table.

---What you intend to do?

---Investigate, take appropriate action.

---That last one's the part that bothers me. Take care.

---You, too, Unc.

He stood to walk me out. As we went around the counter to the hall door, he had his arm around my shoulder. He kept it around me, laughing and talking nonsense in a loud voice, a typical pol, working a constituent in a tone that caused every head to turn and every eye to take note.

I smiled inside. The word was being passed that I was family and I was under his protection and everyone in City Hall would know it before I got off the elevator.

As the elevator door closed on me, he gave a final big wave and boisterous remark, but his eyes were stone serious. I knew what had happened and so did he. He was telling the truth when he said he wouldn't get me off a really heavy rap, but I also knew that I had, at least, his own personal go-ahead to poke around. It was all I wanted for now. Mission accomplished. On both our parts.

I left the lobby for the heat of the plaza. It was still early, so I walked across to the public library. I had never forgiven the city for tearing down the big Greek Revival building on Lee Circle and putting up another glass box. In the old days, you walked up a set of granite steps to enter what was supposed to be, and was, a temple of learning. There was the circular dark wood desk with frowning librarians who could find anything you wanted and there were dark, crowded stacks where you could swim in musty books in ill-lit corridors, dive below crumbling bindings and musty, browning pages, and come up with your first copy of Shakespeare, or your first copy of Plato's Dialogues, two of the finest dramatists who ever lived.

Maybe the same thing happened in the glass box they put up to replace the grand old library. I hoped so. The new one at least had the John Chase mural behind the circulation desk. It was still a charmer.

I went through the recent back issues of the newspaper, then spent a couple of hours trolling the microfilm files to refresh my mind on the players. I can't say I learned anything constructive, but I did let enough time elapse so that I could go back to the theatre expecting to see the staff busily at work. I mean, Don, of course. Of course.

CHAPTER FIVE

On the long, hot walk from the library to the theatre, neatly tucked away on a side street in the Quarter, I tried to tell myself I was heading there because I wanted to see how rehearsals were progressing. I owed it to Don as a friend. All right, I also wanted to see the blonde stage manager.

No one was in the lobby, the box office, or the stage area. Somebody had to be around since the place was unlocked, so I went backstage. There were wet paint brushes drying over the janitor's sink and the flowers on the flat looked finished. I could see some of the same vivid use of color I had seen in the portrait at Don's place. She was good. But she wasn't there. I heard a noise from the tiny dressing room so I wandered back to it. She was there and she was as nude as you can be while wearing clothes.

Bent over the wash basin, hips canted back to me, she had turned a hose on herself to wash off paint spatters. The cascading water plastered the t-shirt to her chest and I could see she didn't wear a bra. My heart started sending out Morse code---"Turn around, turn around." Her hair was wet, her eyes were closed, her head was tilted back and she was so beautiful a lump formed in my throat that could have cut off my air supply forever. I wouldn't have cared. I had seen the best heaven had to offer and I was ready to go.

Luminous is an awfully fancy word to use, but I can't think of a better one. There was only one overhead bulb on, but it picked her out better than any baby spotlight ever could. The water running over her fair skin gave it a pearly sheen and turned her hair dark, but it was obvious from the color, a mix of gold, blonde, and brown with a red highlight that this was no dye job. She was a real blonde. One day I hoped to find that out for certain. From my angle, I could just see the bulge of her bosom as she moved. The water was obviously cold, or perhaps her breasts always stood at attention. I was ready to salute too. In a way, I was.

Unfortunately, I was rudely disturbed by a request.

---When you get finished staring, hand me the towel by the mirror.

Her eyes were closed so I haven't the faintest idea how she knew I was there. She may have heard my heart pounding in my chest. It felt loud enough. On the other hand, she didn't say I had to stop looking, so I got her the towel, figuring that would buy me a few more seconds.

The towel was a threadbare, green terry number that had been used for everything from taking off makeup, to mopping up spills, to cleaning paint off hands. Right then I envied it more than any cloth ever woven, because it was about to caress something I would have given my life savings, if I had any, to touch.

---Now get out while I dry off.

She still had the wet top on so I didn't know how she was going to do get dry. I could have offered to help, but I left. Any southern gentleman would honor such a request from a lady.

I didn't go far. She might have needed another towel, and I wanted to be nearby if she called. I thought it best to stand just outside the dressing room door. At an angle. So I could see inside. In case she went mute and had to signal by hand. I certainly wasn't there to ogle. Besides, she was safe from my direct gaze. I couldn't see anything. Except the mirror that ran the length of the room.

The bulbs around it illuminated the room very well. They had to so the actors could put on their make up before a show and take it off after the show. The mirror was large. It had to be large because many actors shared it. From where I was standing, the mirror did its job, presenting a panoramic view of the dressing room. It was mere happenstance that a wet stage manager stood center stage.

I watched carefully. If I ever turned a hose on myself in a dressing room, I wanted to be sure I toweled off afterward in the correct fashion. These little things are important. She dried her face first, and then brushed the towel through her hair to get the water out. I don't know why she had to turn her back to slip off her shirt. She had no reason to turn around. She had no reason to think anyone was watching, least of all a gentleman like me. She surely knew I wasn't one to crane my head around the corner to gawk at her.

Besides, I didn't have to. The mirror did the job for me. I watched as she ran that lucky towel over her bosom. I should have gotten a smaller towel, because that one covered far too much of her. I saw her eyes flick to the mirror a couple of times, so I suspected she was watching me watching her. I wasn't, really. I was in church, thanking the All High for putting her in the world, and for giving me the opportunity to appreciate His handiwork. OK, maybe I was watching her just a little. I would have been a fool not to. Since she hadn't said anything, I figured she didn't mind and I didn't mind that she didn't mind.

Eventually, she stopped toweling off, though I thought I saw a damp spot or two which I would have gladly toweled for her. The towel she draped over her shoulders hung down to her waist. Next time, I definitely had to hand her a smaller towel.

She turned to me with a smile. Delicious possibilities flooded my mind as I framed the witty words that would win her. Before I could speak them, or even get an unencumbered look at her breasts, she hit me across the face with a two by four. OK, it was only her hand, but it felt like a two by four.

---Next time, ask permission, she said. ---I'm not a Playboy centerfold

If I thought I could have gotten permission I would have asked right then, but since I figured it would only get me another shot in the mouth, I didn't. I had learned how hard she could hit with that delicate-seeming hand. On the other hand, I was still in the presence and, if she wanted to hit me again, I wouldn't have cared as long as I could still look.

---Understand? she asked.

---Yes, sir, I said.

I think I saw a smile on her lips as she turned away, draped the towel on the bar by the sink, picked up a dry top and put it on. I think that's what she did. It was hard to say. My vision had a film of tears over it. Wonderful, round, pink shapes floated before me as I desperately blinked away the tears to restore sight.

---Don's not here, she said.

---Wasn't looking for Don.

---Exactly what were you looking for, or did you see what you came to see, troglodyte?

---Bonuses are nice, but I came here looking for you. 'At you' was a lagniappe.

----I see. Did you like the 'at?'

--Yes, and no. I only got to see your t-shirt. Any chance of a more complete view?

Her hand started up, but, since I respect the power of a stage manager, now more than ever, I ducked for cover. I must have looked pretty silly because her hand went down and she suppressed a smile.

--- And you were looking for me because?

---Lunch.

---It's too late for lunch.

---Then, anything that serves whatever meal is proper so long as I can eat it across the table from you.

---Any place I like?

---Any place, any food, any time.

---OK. Let me lock up and we'll go to my favorite spot to eat.

---Works for me.

We went down the street from the theatre and turned onto Chartres Street. It wasn't too far from Jackson Square and I got worried that we were going to some touristy place. Even though my pockets were fairly empty, I wasn't concerned that I would have to welsh on the meal. That's why God invented credit cards. I just didn't want to eat in the presence of tourists. They were bad for my digestion.

The Quarter was busy with said tourists, clogging the streets and the sidewalks. The cars tried their best to negotiate the streets without hitting them. I felt almost sorry for this big black one. With us from the time we left the theatre, I figured him for a lost tourist because he just couldn't make any headway. I lost sight of him from time to time and thought he'd found his way, but a block or so later he was back. Some people shouldn't be allowed on the streets.

We passed through the pigeons in front of the Cathedral, the winged ones scrabbling for bits of food, not the ones lined up by the wrought iron fences to buy art and have their fortunes told. We skirted a couple of street musicians. In case you wondered, there's a reason some of them are playing on the street and not in a club. On the other hand, I once stood transfixed for thirty minutes while a guy played a solo trombone and made the most beautiful music ever to come out of an instrument that usually reminded me of a certain flatulent basset hound.

We turned up Conti Street and I started to feel better about where we were going to eat. Soon we cleared most of the tourist area and I was looking forward to an interesting little off the beaten track kind of place much like Buster Holmes used to be before he got himself "discovered."

My anxiety level rose again when we turned down a narrow alley that had a sagging brick wall on one side, and the leaning paint-flaking side of a house on the other. I wondered if my friend Doctor Jimmy Hong had a good cure for ptomaine poisoning in his little black bag.

---Where are we going? I asked, trying to keep a quaver out of my voice.

---My apartment, she said.

Instantly, I wondered if I was about to get incredibly lucky.

---No, she said, --- you're not going to get lucky. All you're going to get is a meal.

How'd she *do* that? But then, I guess it wasn't a tremendous leap of deduction. I was probably as obvious as a prom date in the back of a limo.

---I do have money to buy you a meal, you know. Not all broke actors are broke.

---I'm cooking.

---You don't have to.

---Yes, I do. I'm vegetarian. My favorite restaurant is closed at this hour. In the time I have, it would be too hard to find a place to eat that wasn't cluttered with tourists. Veggies OK with you?

---I come from a large, poor family. I will eat anything that doesn't eat me first.

She led me to what are usually called slave quarters in New Orleans but was probably, and more prosaically, a former stable behind the house. As I was closing the gate that big ass car passed by. I wish I had a map to give him, but I was a stranger here myself. Though I hoped the house I was about to go into would become a more regular stop on my road.

The alley widened out to a small cleared area that couldn't be called a patio, though someone had planted a few flowers and shrubs in buckets along the fence. There was even a kind of fishpond rigged with a garden hose and an old wash tub.

---In here, she said, unlocking the right side of a set of French doors.

The door opened into a tiny area that had a kitchen to the left and stairs to the right. Around the corner of the stairs, I could see what I guessed was the living room because it held a sofa, television, bean bag chair, and coffee table. There was an arch by the window across the room which led to another area.

---This is a great place. Don must pay you a whole lot more than I thought he could afford.

Her chin set.

---I pay my way, she said, a layer of ice hanging over every syllable.

I assumed that I was getting a little too personal for our brief acquaintance. But then, I intended our acquaintance to be anything but brief. Something told me that it would be good to drop the subject and also good to give her a little space, so I did both.

---Can I explore?

---That won't take long. You're in the kitchen. That's the sitting area, through it a little room I use as a study.

---What's upstairs? I asked.

---My bedroom, which you are not going to see.

---I never dreamed.

---Of course, you did, but I'm not a wind-up doll

---I know you're not. Sorry.

---Stop with the waif eyes. Stretch out on the couch while I cook.

She started pulling out pans and I walked through the sitting area to scope out the study. There were a lot of books on the walls. It is said that you can tell a lot about someone from the books they read. I flunked. All I learned from her bookcases was that she was interested in everything under the sun

I stole a look into the kitchen. She was bent over to do something in the oven, so I sneaked up the stairs. Telling me not to do something is like bleeding in front of a shark.

Upstairs was a loft with little more than room enough for a bed and a chest of drawers. She was not a neat housekeeper. There were clothes strewn everywhere. Obviously washing day was at hand. Or should be. I checked out the color of her underwear. Pastels. Nice.

Overhead, there was a skylight that was probably the reason she had the apartment, because the light was great. She didn't need much room downstairs, because this was where she spent most of her time. There were paintings everywhere: hanging, leaning, stacked and piled, finished, half-finished, quarter-finished, sketched, begun, and abandoned. They all showed the same vibrant use of color that the painting over Don's couch exhibited.

A lot of them seemed to be of the person on Don's wall. I leaned in to study the one on the easel more closely.

---My brother, a voice behind me said.

Caught. But I maintained a level tone, even as I prepared to get bitch-slapped on the back of my head.

---You paint him a lot.

---I need to. I don't want to forget him.

---He's dead?

The atmosphere resumed its glacial cast. I gently removed my foot from my mouth. At least I wasn't so dumb as to try to say anything more. I kept quiet and waited. She was silent a moment then, drew the flat of her hand across her eyes.

The light filtering from above slanted across the painting and her face. I couldn't see what it did to the painting, but it did wonderful things to her cheekbones. When she put the painting down, there was a glitter of tears in eyes that looked more golden and mysterious than ever.

---It's still not right.

She turned the picture to the wall.

---It will be.

---How do you know that?

--- I think you'll stay with it until it *is* right.

Her head ducked and I couldn't tell if I'd pleased her or made her mad. Anyway, her face pinked, so I wasn't being ignored.

She folded her arms and tried to scowl at me. I never saw the scowl, because folding her arms lifted her breasts to greater prominence.

---I thought I told you not to come up here.

---Not true. You said I would never see it.

---You made a liar of me.

---Not really. I made a snoop out of me, but that's who I am. I like the color of your underwear, by the way.

She flushed and started grabbing at the clothes draped everywhere.

---Don't worry. I have sisters. I've seen underwear before.

---Not mine.

She madly gathered everything in sight and stuffed them into a pillowcase which she took into the small bathroom. I took the opportunity to sprawl on the bed as I watched. She did the arms folded thing when she saw me. I loved what it did to her torso.

---Making yourself at home?

---I'm just a little tired.

---You don't look tired.

---You do. Why don't you stretch out for a minute?

---Why?

---Because it hurts my neck to look up at you.

She moved slowly to the bed and gingerly sat on one corner of it.

---Lord, you're so obvious. You're not getting ideas above your station, are you? she asked.

I reached for her elbow and turned her to me. She moved

slowly, looking at me sideways from those spectacular, slanted eyes. I guess my face got a little funny because her look softened.

---What? she asked in a gentle voice.

---I just think you're the most spectacular thing I ever saw.

I think she liked it, but her eyebrow arched.

---Right. And who haven't you said that to?

---I've never meant it more.

I lay flat on my back across the bed, feet hanging over the edge. She sat for a moment, then leaned on one elbow and drew her legs onto the bed. She reached for my hair and ruffled it across my forehead. I didn't do a thing or say a word. She seemed to relax a little and played with my hair quietly. I watched the face of a small girl playing with a doll. I was more than happy to be the doll.

Her hand stopped and she turned away. I didn't know what she was feeling, so I waited to find out. When her head turned to me again, she looked at me with heavy eyes. I had one brief insight as to what her face would look like when she was making love.

---Well done, she said. ---you got into my bed.

---And on the first date.

---First date, nothing. Within twenty-four hours of meeting me. I never thought I was so easy.

---I seriously doubt that you are.

We looked at each other for a very long time. I reached a hand to stroke her face. She turned her cheek into my hand to return my caress with her face. Dropping her head, she lay back on the bed with her head pillowed on one arm. I rolled across the bed to stretch out on my elbow next to her. We looked at each other, and I traced the line of her face down her neck to her chest, my fingers making a broad circle that almost, but not quite, touched the under slopes of twin mounds rising from the plain of her belly. Her eyes were glinting with amusement though she kept her face stern.

---I'm guessing you have something in mind.

Well, I already knew what her slap was like, and I didn't think she could get a good kick at my crotch from a reclining position, so I told the truth.

---I was wondering how we would fit together.

We lay without moving for a time. I kept my eyes on hers. Or rather, I allowed myself to sink into her eyes and, when I was about drowned, she gently rolled over to lie atop me.

---I don't know why I'm doing this...

I don't believe I'd ever fit together so well with anyone in my life. When she moved ever so slightly atop me, all my teeth fell out. She let the smile lighten her face.

---That's some smooth line you've got, mister, she said. Leaning forward caused her to massage my body with every inch of her own.

When I could breathe without stuttering, I swore on every Bible ever printed.

---It's not a line.

Her endlessly evil eyes looked into mine a long moment. Wrapping her in my arms, I rolled over so I was prone atop her. She gave a gasp and I thought I was going to get hit again but, after a minute, she seemed to soften. She laid her cheek on mine and we flowed together for a few seconds.   It was almost like she decided something, though she didn't say anything. She studied my face and the gold in her eyes gleamed with fire, then, faded to a dull ember. When she spoke, the playful tone was gone.

---Don't get too attached to the idea of you and me.

---Why not?

Her hands went to my chest, not pushing away, but as a barrier.

---You frighten me. Maybe I frighten myself.

I thought about that for a minute then lifted her chin. I tried to pour every ounce of me into my look and then gave the sincerest line reading of my life.

---I would never hurt you.

For a second she wavered between belief and denial and, in the end, opted for neither. Instead, she returned to playful.

---You're lying on top of me.

I brought my hands to her hair and ran my fingers through the wonderful blondeness, letting one finger trace down onto that sculpted cheek and playing under the upward angle of her eye.

---You feel nice.

---Well, you're certainly trying to "feel" me.

She moved under me. It may have been by accident, but I hoped not. It was like getting the world's best body massage and it took away my capacity for speech even as it excited my capacity for other things.

---You know what I want? I asked, trying for a lighter tone.

---I can tell what you want, and you're not going to get it, she said, bumping upward with her hips and laughing.

I was caught. Well, what did you expect? She was desirable and I was human. I did have to admit it was something of a breach of good manners. On the other hand, it could be considered a compliment, too.

---Ignore that, I said. ---Everyone else does.

Her eyes crinkled at the corners and a smile spread across her face. She reached a hand to bring my head very close to her face.

---Why do I doubt that? she said into my ear.

I went into tachycardia and had to make a conscious decision to remain adult and not break into a ceaseless goo-goo-ing that might have lowered my masculine status in her eyes, even if it was what I felt like doing. I stayed with witty remarks.

---You know, you brought me here on false pretenses. You promised me food but you lured me into your bedroom.

---I told you to stay out of my bedroom.

---What better way to get me in here?

We smiled at each other, and I gave her a very small peck on the cheek. I would like to think she debated making passionate love to me for a second, but life is full of disappointment. In the end, we each got to our feet and walked to the stairs. In the doorway, I turned to the bed.

---I'll be back, I said.

She blushed as she left. She was halfway down the stairs before I realized something. Maybe her face got redder, but she hadn't disputed me and that made me feel really, really good.

---You didn't say no.

---I didn't, did I?

We had burgers of Portobello mushroom sautéed with red pepper and onion on phyllo bread. They were delicious. They were not as delicious as lying in her bed, but what can you expect of mere food.

CHAPTER SIX

We left as soon as we ate. I offered to do the dishes, but she recognized it for the cheap ploy to prolong our time together that it was. It was heading toward evening, and she said she had to get back to the theatre. I made a mental note to tell Don he worked her too hard.

She wouldn't let me walk her all the way, so we parted on the corner of Conti and Chartres. We didn't kiss; we didn't shake hands; we just looked at each other, then she turned to walk away. I stood watching, of course. There are some things in life you simply do not pass up. I was wondering if she knew I was watching. Then she cast that half glance over her shoulder and that made me very happy as I walked uptown to catch the Magazine Street bus.

Parasol's is not much to look at, and there are far more attractive bars up near the university. The clientele was working class people from the Irish Channel. Except for St. Patrick's Day when it hosted the parade and served green beer, there were only two reasons to go there. They served the best roast beef poor boys ever made, and you could get any information you needed if you were willing to invest a few dollars in beer and a few hours buying them for Red John.

No one ever took Red John's seat, so he was at the end of the bar when I walked in. If you ever had any doubt whether or not you were talking to Red John, all you had to do was look at his face. It looked like the worst case of sunburn you ever saw, but it wasn't. It was just Red John.

He had worked the streets as a cop for thirty years and he had worked this bar for the last twenty. He didn't work *at* the bar. He just worked the bar for drinks from opening to closing. The owner never complained. Why should he? He was making a fortune.

Everyone thought Red John's great skill was talking. Not true. He was a world class listener. He told you his stories and you loosened up, thinking he was a clown, and the first thing you knew, you were telling him things you wouldn't tell a priest in confession. Especially things you wouldn't tell a priest in confession.

That was why Red John had a lot of friends. It wasn't that Red John was the village washerwoman, spreading gossip down at the corner grocery. It was just that Red John stored all that information away. His use of it varied. If you were reluctant to buy him a drink, he might hint at something you told him that your wife, boss, mother, girlfriend, police chief, tax collector, and bookie would like to know, and that you most positively would not want them to know. Cops loved him because he could help finger a perp faster than he could down a beer, and housewives loved him because he knew what their husbands were doing when they weren't home. Perps also loved him because he wouldn't finger anybody who was keeping to their side of the street because, after all, a man had a family to feed, and husbands loved him because he was an early warning system that let them know when it was time to stop their wandering ways and cleave to the family bosom. The result was that everyone was happy and Red John had not had to pay for a beer in years.

I don't know that Red John ever spent a nickel of his pension. Why should he? Everyone was willing to pick up his tab to get him to talk, or to keep him from talking. If there was something you wanted to know, you had to know how to appeal to the finer aspects of Red John's nature.

---Buy you a beer? I asked.

---Is the pope Jewish?

---No.

---Then, I'll have one.

---Suppose I'd said yes?

---I still would've had one.

Red John emptied the beer on essentially one long pull then looked quizzically at me. I signaled for another, He smiled in satisfaction. Red John knew a pigeon when one fluttered to sit on the bar stool next to him. I waited until his beer came and he emptied half of it, which did not take as long to do as it does to say. He went for another swallow, but I stopped his hand. I was not made of money.

---You knew my father?

---A fine man.

---Any idea what he was up to there at the end?

---A man couldn't say, though he did seem interested in those deserted shacks they been buying up to build that thing that looks like Disneyland South

Red John kept his eyes fixed on the mirror where he could see my eyes, even if his seemed to be staring up at one of the parasols overhead.

---Been a lot of fires in those deserted building. Lot of fires in some buildings what ain't yet deserted.

---Know anything about the way he died?

--A tragic accident, it's said.

---What do you say?

Red John finished the beer, the drinking of which I had so rudely interrupted, gave a satisfied belch, and looked at me again. I waved at the bartender who already had another on its way. Did I mention that Red John was a regular at the place?

---I'd say, if I was to say anything, and I'm not a man who has a lot to say, I'd say, if I was asked, that I don't know.

I scooped up the bills on the counter and got up.

---Then I guess I'd leave.

A vise clasped onto my hand before I could get my legs under my butt. The huge red blob that was Red John's face came close to mine.

---But I might know someone who might know.

I sat down and looked into the mirror. I wanted to see if Red John's breath had taken layers of epidermis off my face. It hadn't. I turned to him and jingled the change in my pocket. He grew expansive.

---In fact, it could be safely said, I'd say, that this fellow might have something to say on the subject, or so it's said.

Maybe you followed that. I wasn't sure I had. In a foolish effort to cut to the heart of the matter, I betrayed my complete ignorance of the finer points of the art of conversation by asking a direct question.

---And his name?

---I'd have to think.

I pulled out a wad of bills and wished I'd had more than a Portobello mushroom sandwich and foreplay before I'd gone there. It was going to be a long night, and I needed some ballast to get me through the evening.

---Gimme a roast beef poor boy dressed, and heavy on the gravy, I said.

I lifted an eye in Red John's direction, knowing all the while it was a foolish hope.

---I'll have another beer, Red John said.

It was already on its way. Like I said, Red John was a regular and he was helping put the bartender's kids through Redemptorist Elementary School down the street.

The roast beef was great, but it always was. After I ate and swabbed the bar, the stool, the floor, and the people sitting on either side of me—I had asked for a lot of gravy—I got the silly idea that if I kept pace with Red John, I might wear him down. I had been away far too long. Through an increasingly alcoholic haze, I began to realize I really should have done more drinking to train for this conversation, though I did manage to get a few things out of Red John.

One of the things that I found of interest was that the week before my father's death a stranger had come into the bar and tried to pry information about my father out of Red John. This was a futile effort, Red John said, because he was a close-mouthed man.

I wanted to know what he looked like, but description was not Red John's strong point. I was looking for someone who looked like either Finn McCool or Pee Wee Herman.

Item two was that a young, hot shot detective had drawn the investigation into my father's last days, but had been bumped off it by persons unknown.

The third thing was that, though the official finding was that it was a tragic accident, there was some suggestion from mysterious, but forceful, quarters that nobody, repeat, nobody, should say or think otherwise. This last was accompanied by a look from blue eyes, as direct as the bore of a rifle, pointed right at my nose.

---I guess it'd be foolish to look into it, then, I said.

He turned back to the mirror and his eyes got a misty look that anyone who didn't know him would take for inebriation.

---You wouldn't have much between your belt and your knees if you didn't, he said.

I raised a glass to my lips and caught his eye in the mirror. I've got a pretty fair ear for the sound of a human voice, and I gave Red John a sample.

---I'd say, if I was to say anything, and I'm not a man who has a lot to say, I'd say, if I was asked, that I think you're right.

His voice dropped to a level that only I could hear and the happy innocuous drunk disappeared to show the street-wise cop who had put in his thirty years on some of the meanest streets in the city.

---I'd say, if I was to say anything, and I'm not a man who has a lot to say, I'd say, that you might better be getting onto it.

I gave a slight nod and drained my glass.

---I think I will.

Red John emptied his beer and picked up one of the two that were standing there waiting for him, his prodigious thirst being legendary in the neighborhood, and a source of great profit for the bar.

---How many eyes you got? he asked.

---Most people get by with two, I said.

---Most people are not Nosy Parkers stepping out of their league.

---How many might such a person need?

---At least two more in the back of his head.

I wet my lips with the beer that had magically appeared at my elbow and searched for stray bits of roast beef gravy on the plate without much success. I had done a pretty good job of sopping it up earlier. Damn, it was good.

---I'd say, if I was to say anything, and I'm not a man who has a lot to say, I'd say that I was grateful for the suggestion.

---You're welcome.

---I'd be more grateful for a suggestion as to where those eyes should be looking.

---That I wouldn't say. But I do meet a lot of politicians in here.

---Any special office.

---Oh, all shapes and sizes. Judges are regulars around here. Some as would like to buy me a beer and some as I wouldn't have a beer from them if I was dying of thirst in the middle of the desert at noon in summer with the entire British army after me.

---Would one of these have a name?

---I couldn't say.

What Red John could and could not and would and would not say was getting very muddled in my head, but if there was a judge around who was so big a SOB that Red John wouldn't take beer from him, that was an interesting judge. There was one way to try to pry it out of him and I gave it a shot.

---Need more beer?

---I didn't say I couldn't say. I said I wouldn't say. There's a lot of beer in the world and I intend to try to drink it all before I go.

Interesting. Damn interesting. Not only that I might need to be careful, I would have been that anyway, but that there was information that couldn't be pried out of Red John by beer. I turned my head to the mirror and studied the image of the two of us. Red John closed one eye in a slow and deliberate wink and nodded. My blood ran just that little bit colder. I'd got what I had come for. Not all of it, but more than I had before and more than I really wanted to know.

I decided to call it a night. Pete the bartender wanted to call a cab for me, but, since the bus stop was only a block away, I said I would take the bus.

Red John was not a great one for farewells. When I left, he was already deep in conversation with what looked to be a university kid and his date out for local color. There were several things I was certain of as I went out the door:

1) the kid was going to be poorer when he left;
2) he was not going to make class the

following day; and,

    3) his date was going to be groped.

Red John had a reputation.

The night was pretty black outside. The trees from the yards in front of the camelback houses with gingerbread trim cast big shadows across the sidewalk. When the air hit me, so did the beer and I wished I had taken Pete up on the cab.

I was making good progress by bouncing off the iron spike fences into the cars parked along the curb and then back again. I was covering a lot of ground. More ground in fact than the distance from the bar to the bus stop, but, what the hell, it was a nice night for walking.

That changed when a pair of arms grabbed me from behind and smashed my face into the hood of the nearest car. It was a Honda. I knew, because the emblem was pressed into my cheek when I got home. There must have been at least two guys, because one held me and the other used my ribs as a weight bag. He threw some pretty fair combination shots, I had to admit.

I let my knees sag to give him the idea that he was winning—he was—and when the guy holding me relaxed just a bit, I thrust upward, using the big muscles in butt and thighs to get a lot of kinesthetic force working for me. My head made a satisfactory crack against his chin and he let go my arms.

I threw a punch in the direction of his groin and turned for the other guy who had not spent the evening in pleasant conversation with Red John, and, consequently, had a lot less in his stomach than I did. He proved it by moving a whole lot faster than me and getting all his body behind the fist that caught me full in the stomach, proving once and for all that beer tastes better going down than coming up.

There was a commotion in the direction of the bar followed by a scream and the sound of running feet. My dance partners left while I still had space on my card. I wasn't hurt by their defection. I hated the steps they had shown me. Around this time, getting rid of the rest of the beer seemed like a good idea, so I did. Most of it went on the Honda

The running footsteps stopped in front of me with a gagging sound. No fair. I was the one who thought of vomiting first.

---How disgusting, said a female voice.

I couldn't disagree, but it seemed rude to say so, given my circumstances.

---You OK? said a young male voice.

---Thanks to you I will be.

I turned to study the couple from the bar. Their evening had been shorter than I thought it would be. Red John was losing his touch.

---Leaving so soon? I asked.

---That disgusting old man put his hand under my dress, the girl said.

---You're lucky that's all he put under your dress.

I kept my head out the window on the drive to let the wind blow on my face, and to guard against a further social gaffe. I had them drop me a block from Don's apartment. I wanted to walk a little before I went in.

It hadn't been a bad evening. I was the recipient of a delightful beating, delightful because it indicated that someone was reluctant to have me proceed. If someone did not want me to proceed, then there was something to be found. If there was something to be found, then I was right to look into my father's death. If I was right to look into his death, then, perhaps, there was more behind it than what was said. If there was someone behind my father's death, I could crush his spleen when I found him. All I had to do was find him.

CHAPTER SEVEN

The docks were our playground growing up. It was easy to get past the guards, the longshoremen didn't care, and there were just so damned many places to hide in the dark corners. The pilings under the docks made for a great jungle gym set with the water there to accidentally fall into on hot days.

I also loved the docks for the romance of it.

People usually laugh when I say that, but those boats from all those places I read about in books took me to another, wider world. The incredible sounds of the various languages, the strange shipments offloaded from the huge boats, the smells of coffee and bananas and the burnt rubber smell of the forklifts as they shuttled pallets around the echoing gray wharf buildings, and the cool smell of the river, scented with who knew what made it a great place to explore, and play, and dream, and those three words define me as well as any in the language.

It was around lunch time when I got there. The work gangs had just knocked off. A few machines were being parked, a few clocks were being punched, and a few hits were being taken out of bottles that weren't supposed to be there, but who wanted to run their hands into a sweat-soaked shirt to search? They were about to scatter to eat or drink their lunch, so I hurried to catch up with them. I didn't want to wander in the dark and I didn't want to miss the guy I had come to see.

I didn't have to worry. I spotted him right away. A group was smoking over by the timekeeper's shack and a very large black shape towered above the others. He seemed about three times as big as I remembered him, and I had thought as a kid that he was a giant. Out of that perverse streak that has kept me from financial security and in physical danger for much of my life, I called out as loudly as I could.

---Big Black Paul Bunyan around?

He turned with a speed surprising for a man his size, but then, most big men can move fast. It just depends on whether they carry muscle or fat. It was all muscle with him. Belatedly I hoped he remembered me. I hoped he could still take a joke. I hoped he still liked me. I hoped my Equity hospitalization was in effect. The men around him backed away from what, they thought, was an approaching, and very bloody, confrontation.

A few slow steps and a raising of his shoulders brought him to me. More properly, above me, for he truly was a big man. He pushed his sleeves up forearms the size of small Volkswagens and folded his right fist into his left hand.

Around me I could hear the unspoken prayers of the assembly as they mentally chipped in to buy a funeral wreath for the new idiot in town.

---Little Hammer, he smiled.

To the sound of jaws dropping to the concrete floor, I moved into a gigantic abrazo which could have suffocated me had I not been expecting it. He put me down and I launched a little jab to his gut. It bounced off like a handball against a concrete wall.

I remembered to thank Saint Genesius that he still knew who I was. My father was the Big Hammer. I was the Little Hammer, not because I was built like my father, I sure as hell wasn't, but because I was his shadow who tagged along with him whenever I could.

---Long time, big scary black man.

---Back to you, scrawny white dude.

We shook hands and he threw an arm around my shoulder. He turned to the loading gang standing around.

---This here's my little brother. Don't nobody mess with him, hear.

At the moment, I could have run for Pope with that crowd and been elected. The whistle blew and they shuffled out the door.

---You hungry? I asked.

---Is the Pope Baptist?

---No, he's not.

---Would be if he had any sense. Let's eat.

All fire fighters work second jobs. Most teachers and policemen do, too. Why the hell we pay the people who provide the most service the least amount of money is a rant for another day. My father had done his time on the riverfront. He had a family to support and doing that almost killed him.

If it had, I don't think it would have bothered him—except for not getting to see his kids and grandkids grow up. His idea of being a man was relatively simple—you took care of your family, and you didn't cry about your lot in life.

My dad had worked with Paul, whose last name was not Bunyan, but who was big enough to deserve the name, and, in the easy social life of New Orleans, they had been friends. It always amazed me that the politicians were so eager to separate people who basically got along just because their skin was different shades and colors. It was my father's opinion that black and white mattered less than rich and poor because poor people knew from their wallets that they shared the same concerns and problems and working together was the solution. They try not to say that in elections because you get votes by dividing people. It may be idiotic, but it works every time.

I never knew Paul's background any more than he knew mine. We shared a bond we discovered by accident the day he refused to kill a rat on the docks. Some fool asked if he was afraid and he said, "not of the rat" and when the idiot pressed him, he got in the guy's face and said --" I like killin' too much." And then he looked right at me. We never talked about it. We never needed to.

The restaurant we went to was right off the wharves and had none of the décor you associate with the French Quarter, even though it was on its fringe. Décor is for tourists. A restaurant is a place to eat and you want food hot, good, and relatively inexpensive. If you can do that you don't need plastic Spanish moss and *papier mache* bricks.

This place had a cement floor, wooden picnic benches and bare brick walls. It was as noisy as a boiler factory and, between the densely packed bodies waiting to eat and Papa Jack's stoves, as heated as a sauna, but it did a great business because the food was hot, good, and relatively inexpensive.

Papa was, in fact, on the premises. He was dark as a bowling ball and about as round. He ate his own food and was the best possible advertisement for his cooking. If you liked his food and told him so, you were his friend. If you didn't like his food but ate it anyhow, you were a customer. If you complained about his food, you were a candidate for the cadaver tank at Charity Hospital.

We sat at the table and Paul flashed some finger signs at Papa Jack who nodded, wrote on a piece of paper, and handed it through the window into the kitchen. The menu was not huge, and the regulars knew the numbers of the orders, so they just signaled them to Papa who had it filled and brought to you. It was a very efficient system. It was also a rite of passage.

When your signal was accepted, you were a regular. If your signal was ignored for a long time before it was finally acknowledged, you were a customer and you had better do something to get on Papa's good side. If you had to wait for a waitress to come to the table to take your order, you were someone who would be well-advised to eat elsewhere.

A waitress placed two longneck bottles of Barq's on the table as she passed by with a tray of shrimp poor boys. Incidentally, don't ever refer to Barq's as a root beer. It is technically sarsaparilla. But if you have any questions about it, you are probably not a native and I don't know if you should be drinking it.

Paul looked around the room from his great height, not only because he was tall, but also because he was the baddest bastard in the room. I'll tell you how badass he was. He didn't have to prove it.

Two trenchers that could have handled a roast pig were placed in front of us along with two bibs and a roll of paper towels. If you don't need bibs and paper towels to eat your roast beef poor boy, it is not an authentically New Orleans roast beef poor boy. If you don't like your roast beef sandwich swimming in gravy, stay in Kansas.

We ate what would be a year's rations for a Third World army in silence. Papa's poor boys did not fill you up, they satiated you. There were those who said Papa's poor boys were better than sex, not having had either for far too long, I couldn't judge. Anyway, we finished and there was a huge amount of roast beef gravy on our chins and the barest sprinkle of crumbs on the plates. I was as satisfied as a person could be who wasn't watching someone turn a hose on herself in a dressing room.

Paul pushed back from the table and fished a toothpick out of the shot glass on the table. While he explored his molars, I ran over what I knew about him. When you saw him, you wondered why he wasn't a guard for the Saints, but he had never been into sports. In fact, his favorite pastime was cooking and he was damned good. I always thought he should open a restaurant, but he could never be confined to a kitchen. He needed space around him. He filled the docks, but, if he stepped out on the river side, he came into contact with something as elemental as him. He and my dad were friends. That meant I was draped in the same mantle.

---Why you back, Little Hammer?

I had always wished more people called me Little Hammer. Carrying a name like Jeffrey around has been a burden at times.

---My dad died.

---He's buried.

---But is he sleeping easy?

---You think he's not?

I tried to put it into words that would make sense, maybe to me as much as him. People kept asking me that question and I had no really solid answer to give them. My real reason is that my father once told me that if he was ever found dead in a locked room, with a rope around his neck, a gun in his hand, a bottle of poison by his side, and a suicide note in what was indisputably his own handwriting, I was to do one thing, and that was to find the son-of-bitch who murdered him.

That he died an accidental death was hard to swallow. Yeah, accidents happen and all of us die. I just wanted to be sure beyond doubt that he went to meet his Maker in his own time. You see, one day I'm going to pass through that great proscenium in the sky. I'm not afraid to meet my Maker. He knows I've done the best I could. But I positively do not want to find my father looking unhappy when we meet in that ultimate green room. Him, I am afraid of.

---I want to be very sure, I said

---I can appreciate that.

---You knew him as well as anybody and you saw him a lot. Were things OK with him?

He sucked on his teeth for a while, then he killed his Barq's and tilted his chair back to look at me.

---Remember Bubber Watkins?

How could I not? He was my dad's best friend.

---He died.

---I know.

---Hit your dad pretty hard.

That would surprise no one. He was the first friend Dad made when he came to the city and his favorite drinking partner. Paul looked at me with flat, dark eyes.

---Bubba died ugly.

Sometimes I am almost intelligent.

---How ugly?

---That old house he was living in down toward the docks. Space heater was faulty or something. When they carried him out, he looked like he'd been cooked. Everybody blamed the landlord.

---Who owned it?

---Some politician.

---And?

---And after that, your dad seemed real serious. Said Bubba hadn't died in his own time, that somebody helped him over the threshold.

---Did he have anything to go on?

---He said that by the time he was finished he would.

---And?

---I hear that he started keeping strange hours in strange places with strange people.

---Like?

---Never thought to ask. I could find out.

--- Anything else?

---Spent a lot of time at City Hall.

---Unc didn't say anything about that.

---Maybe it wasn't with him.

---What else?

---Started driving around the fire district down by the bridge.

---Looking for?

---Ask at the fire house.

---I will.

---Shot a lot of pool at Bennie's.

---Bennie's.

---You gonna write this down?

---Actors have real good memories.

I swirled the last of my Barq's around, tipped the bottle and my head back to drain it. I had enough suggestions to follow up, that was for sure. I'd probably better get started. Paul was looking at me very intently. Paul looking at you intently is enough to seize your colon for a week.

---You think something's wrong about all this.

---I think I need to find out.

---If something does come down, let me know.

--- Will Paul Bunyan bring his axe?

---Hell, I'll bring Babe the Big Blue Ox.

We did another abrazo that cracked my spine and improved my posture and he left. I watched him go across the railroad tracks to the docks. If ever I went into harm's way, I would want Paul with me. He looked bulletproof. I couldn't be sure I was.

CHAPTER EIGHT

The next day, I slept in. Around 11:00 a.m. I negotiated some coffee and an English muffin with orange marmalade. I would have to buy Don more muffins soon. The orange marmalade's vendor was a secret. After eating, I decided I would live, so I showered, dressed, and resisted the temptation to pass by the theatre to check on... Well, to check.

I caught the Magazine Street bus again, which was getting to be my transportation of choice, and headed uptown.

When I was a kid, I thought the police precinct in the neighborhood was a castle. It looked like one. The right-hand corner of the precinct house looked like a turret rising to a green-tinted roof that let you know it was made of copper. The turret had a big bay window. Through the window you could see wainscoting and hardwood floors. The booking desk was so beautiful you could have pulled it out and set it up as a gentleman's bar in the fanciest uptown club.

The precinct house had big steps going up to an arched door inlaid with cut glass panels. At the top of the steps on each side, a tall brass lamp was mounted on the wall. Below it on the top stoop, were two lions carrying shields. Above the door, was another shield with an ornate decoration and a Latin inscription.

I never knew what it said while I was growing up. When I got older, I didn't want to know because we had made up our own inscription which had to do with the Knights Templar and the Holy Grail. If the inscription actually said to leave the laundry at the back door, it would have been too disappointing.

It was a familiar place because my grandfather had put in time there. He was a policeman for thirty years. He always called it "being on the penal force."

Apparently, he was a helluva cop. He never got beyond patrolman, but he knew the streets he was responsible for like the palm of his hand. Once some detectives came to him about a truck that had been broken into behind a shoe store but only left shoes had been stolen. He didn't say a word, just led them to the house where the one-legged ex-con lived.

He was never mad at the perps he arrested, and they never resented him. It was all part of the game that was played. I was always glad he retired before drugs took over the streets. It wouldn't have been the same for him.

None of the younger cops remembered him, but there were still a few of the old guard who did. After he passed, I liked to talk with them. I was always interested in my family.

I walked through the narrow hall bisecting the building to the detective squad room. Nobody was in the room, so I poured myself some three-day old coffee. It was hard to see through the glass of the pot, coffee having been overcooked in it on a daily basis since it came into the building.

The sludge that spilled into the cup had the consistency of crankcase oil which meant it was pretty good for cop house coffee. I wandered over to the window to kill time by looking outside. The playground next to the station had a full complement of children on swings and slides and mothers sitting on benches under the trees, fanning themselves with newspapers in the late summer heat. The sound of children playing is one that is always peaceful no matter how loud they screech. Behind the playground was the branch library. It was a real library, though not as elaborate as the old main branch. There were stairs climbing up the front and big windows that let in a lot of light. I knew that the circulation desk would be large and wooden and the books would have that special aroma that only comes from being touched by a lot of people who actually read them, and quickly put back on the shelves to incubate that smell so the next person to check it out could share in the life of the last person to read it.

It seemed appropriate to have the playground flanked on the other side by the library. I beamed a thought onto the playground. Use that building well, and you might have less need of this one, kids. Everything is experience. If you take the experiences of others that are captured in books and adopt them as your own, you just might get away with paying a lesser price for your stupidities.

There may have been more profundities out there, but about that time a young guy came into the room.

---Help you?

---Looking for the detective who investigated my father's death. Retired firefighter. Found under an overpass with his car on the road above.

---You got him. Who are you?

---A guy who wants to talk about his father's death.

---You're Jeff Chaussier, the actor.

---On a good day.

---I was told you might be by.

---And?

---I was told that I should talk to you.

---Who told you that?

---A gentleman from city hall. A friend?

---Even worse. He's a relative.

---You have any decent seafood lately?

That was an unexpected question, but an appealing one. My stomach started to grumble as soon as he said it.

---None worth eating.

---Let's go across the street to Casamento's.

I knew the place. Best seafood anywhere.

I looked him over as we walked across the street. He had dark eyes and black curly hair, a broad mouth that would smile as easily as it would thin out into a line so fine you couldn't insert paper between his lips. Studying faces is my business. I decided to take a shot on this one.

I have no idea how long Casamento's had been around, certainly as long as I could remember. As you came in, there was a tall white-tiled oyster bar that had green tile borders at the top and bottom. The edge of the counter was built up so you could eat as many raw oysters as you wanted without worrying about the juice slopping onto your shoes.

Louisiana red hot and catsup, Creole mustard and horseradish were within easy reach and the shuckers were lined up behind sinks filled with wet burlap sacks of shellfish waiting to be cracked.

---My treat, I said.

We headed for a back booth. The floor was made up of those small octagonal white tiles with intricate patterns and borders built into it. Damn, they used to know how to build things. Also, the whole place looked easy to keep clean. No small consideration in a place where you eat.

---Ramirez, John.

---Jeff Chaussier.

--- I'm ordering some raw up front.

--- Order what you want.

Damn if he didn't take me up on it. As a citizen, I should have been upset that my tax dollars were being wasted while he stuffed his face. On the other hand, I hadn't paid taxes here for a long time and, since I was going to ask him to bend the law, I might as well have him well-stuffed when I did.

He had two dozen raw plus the seafood platter, gumbo, a Wop salad—it sounds offensive, but that's what they call it in New Orleans—and garlic bread washed down with two Barq's Root Beer. They say it isn't true root beer, but I say to hell with them.

I had the seafood platter and the ethnically incorrect salad with iced tea. We ate without a lot of talk. I doubt that he could have talked anyway, given the way he shoveled it down. Finally, he sat back and explored his molars with a toothpick from the little shot glass on the table.

---Do you think my father's death was an accident?

---No foreplay?

---I bought you a meal.

---Thanks, but I've got to go.

---Sit down or I'll pull those oysters out of your nostrils.

He smiled and settled back into his chair, propping his feet on the seat on my side of the booth.

---If you didn't think it was an accident, why'd you write it that way?

---Didn't. Pulled off the case.

---Why?

---I'd like to know.

---I'd like to find out.

---I was told you would.

---Want to do a little free-lance work with me?

---I want to put in thirty and draw a pension so I can fish for snapper and redfish the rest of my life.

---Can't blame you.

---On the other hand, if I wasn't curious, I'd probably be selling insurance.

---Where would you start? If you weren't a highly ethical future pensioner?

---Autopsy report might be interesting.

---Can I see it?

---No.

That seemed cold. After all, I had just fed him enough to satisfy the Cajun Air Force. Before I could ask that we go Dutch, he restored my faith in seafood as a bribe.

---On the other hand, my desk is a mess. Who knows what might be lying on the top of it, or when I'll get around to doing my filing.

---Can I see your office? I've always wanted to know what a real police place looks like.

He fished another toothpick out of the small glass on the table by the ketchup and hot sauce bottles and searched the spaces between his teeth for anything he had forgotten to swallow.

---Why would you do this? I asked curiously.

---There's a reason I became a cop and thirty and redfish don't explain it all. Also, I got a Latin temper, and I don't like to have a case snatched away from me without an explanation. Most of all I'm nosy.

---You're more than nosy.

---Maybe. But I'd like to do my thirty at the highest grade I can. I'd be able to buy better redfish bait.

--- I might help you to that.

---Or put me on the street with only a cane pole.

I studied him across the table. When you meet somebody good

for a trip down a dark alley with you, it's a nice feeling. I knew he was. I nodded and he nodded back.

---Let's go, I said.

---After coffee.

And he made me sit there while he drank two cups of coffee, with three sugars, and enough evaporated milk to give it the color of a khaki shirt. I hoped his cholesterol levels permitted him to eventually collect that pension

We finally made it to the office. While he was digging for the file, I decided to do a little fishing myself. I didn't dare try to match beer with Red John again, but the thought of a judge who was so big a SOB that Red John wouldn't take beer from him was nagging at me. I waited until I thought Ramirez was distracted by his paper chase. Lord knows, he might need a pick and shovel before he found anything.

---Who's the dirtiest bastard of a judge in town?

---Now, that is a tightly contested competition.

---And the winner is?

He resumed excavating like a miner forty-niner. From under a pile of paper, a dust laden sentence, so low it could barely be heard, floated out.

---Ever met a judge named Duplantis?

---No. Who is he?

His eyes took on a look that told me he had left the office, loaded his rifle, and gone hunting for big game only to be told his license was revoked.

---Fiftyish, thinks he's a devil with the ladies, would steal the nails from Christ on the cross and convict him of public nudity, and he has the morals of a squid.

Actors have expressive faces. But we also play poker to pass the time between cues. I knew this game.

---Should he be a person of interest for me?

For a moment, he let the façade drop and I could tell he was speaking from a place where a thirty-year pension carried no weight.

---No idea. But one day I'm going to nail his sorry sadistic ass.

His low, level, quiet, tone made me lean forward.

---Something personal?

The cop was back and he was as bland as vanilla yogurt.

---My mother raised me to scotch snakes. And he's a big'un.

I thought about it for a minute. I didn't see that it had anything to do with me, but information is information. You gather it, you sort it, and you use what you think fits.

Don't know if it's the best way, but it's the way I know.

I guess I wasn't paying attention because his voice surprised me when he spoke. He gave the folder a final tap and tossed it on the Everest of paper atop his desk.

---Don't see the file. Not that I would let anyone see it, but if I find it and leave it on my desk, I certainly hope no one will read it.

He sauntered casually to the door while I sat, my eyes seemingly closed and my mind wandering after a big meal.

---Think I'll go to the john, he said.

Thirty seconds later, I walked through the children on the playground with a manila file sticking to the perspiration under my shirt.

In my pocket was his card. He had explained that for relaxation he liked to read detective novels because he loved a good mystery and if I came across a good one, I should let him know.

He also said that the limit on library checkouts in the building across the way was three days. I told him I was a fast reader.

In point of actual fact, I had no intention of reading it. I didn't know that I would understand it anyway.

I was raised to believe that you didn't have to know anything in this life. You just had to know who to ask.

There are many doctors in the world with great knowledge and high standards. Those people might question where I had come up with a police autopsy report.

While scientific integrity was a wonderful thing, it might prove an impediment in this case.

On the other hand, there were practitioners with the ethical sensitivity of a pecan. In these cases, their conclusions might be suspect.

No. What I needed was a good doctor with good ethics who would also keep his mouth shut. I needed a doctor who was also a friend and I knew just where to find one.

CHAPTER NINE

The back ramp of Charity Hospital was crowded with police cars and ambulances, which was no surprise. It was probably the busiest trauma unit in the country. The VA hospital across the street was casting a heavy shadow over it as the sun started down the off ramp of the expressway.

I had a warm spot in my heart for Charity. I had clocked a lot of time in it with various childhood diseases, accidents, and misfortunes. I was not at the hospital because of my stupidity this time. If I was going to understand what was in the report, I needed a doctor.

I was here to see Jimmy Hong. Jimmy was the smartest kid in my school. He was a cinch to succeed at whatever he turned his hand to. Jimmy wanted to be a jazz pianist. Unfortunately, his parents determined that he would be a doctor. Jimmy was a very obedient child. I had no doubt that he was a helluva doctor. Working in the emergency room was his bit of rebellion at parents, who had envisioned a posh uptown office and a well-heeled society clientele.

Jimmy had that, too. He was rebellious, not stupid, but working the ER for three shifts a week was his way of claiming a little piece of his soul for himself. I think he always felt a little guilty that things came so easily to him. I didn't think things came easy for him. The pressure he got from his parents would have crippled most people. Jimmy wasn't most people. Maybe his parents did him a favor by imposing the weight of their expectations on him, because Jimmy loved his work. That's why he was in the Emergency Room.

I used to wonder how he kept centered. For a long time, I had the idea that it had to do with his mysterious Oriental heritage. OK. So, I'm an actor and not the most stable person in the world, but it made a certain kind of sense. I shared that with him one day and received the kind of look he'd probably give to something in a petri dish. He told me that if I would meet him after midnight one Friday, he would reveal the source of his serenity.

It was the best damn blues piano I ever heard, at a dingy club

I'd never been to, and I was only mildly surprised when Jimmy was invited to sit in, and then played the wickedest blues licks of the night. When he saw me watching, he almost lost his riff he was laughing so much. Jimmy always had a heightened sense of the ridiculous. That was a good thing to have if you worked the emergency room at Charity.

He was bent over one of the gurneys that normally clog the ward when I showed up. I took the time to watch him work. He had lost a little more hair, which didn't mean much, because he started going bald at the age of eighteen. He claimed it was because his superior brain power used up chemicals that produced hair in lesser men. We claimed it was the pounds of Vaseline he used to slick his hair down. We were all probably right. He looked good in his white coat. It went with his black horned- rimmed glasses. That, and his Asian coloring, made him look like an incredibly wise medical practitioner.

---Doctor Jimmy? I asked.

His hand stopped for just a second, and I could see a smile twitch his lips, but he didn't let on he recognized my voice.

---One minute, grasshopper. I'm busy.

I suppose he was, if suturing the arm of a drunk counted as busy. The drunk probably thought so, since his arm was split from his elbow to his armpit. The floor was littered with red gauze and towels. A nurse kept pouring what looked like alcohol over the open wound as Jimmy sewed industriously.

I could see a lot of muscle and nerves exposed, but the guy never flinched or seemed to notice. Jimmy sewed, and the nurse kept pouring what my nose and eyes told me had to be something terribly astringent over the gaping cut.

---What is that stuff? I asked her.

---Antiseptic.

---Doesn't that hurt? I asked.

---Not if you have as many chemicals in your body as he does, the nurse answered.

---How'd he get cut? I wondered.

---How'd you get cut? Jimmy asked the drunk.

Whatever he mumbled was out of my hearing, but Jimmy just nodded and kept sewing.

---You came in here with your leg split open the last time the Martians tried to kidnap you. Don't you think you'd better stop hanging out with Martians?

The drunk offered quite a lengthy explanation, possibly in Martian, because I know I never understood a word he said. Jimmy kept sewing.

---It's very nice that you saved the planet again, but these Martians are wearing you down. Did you ever think of switching allegiance?

More incoherent mumblings from the drunk and nodding and sewing from Jimmy.

---No, I don't think so. The last time you hung out with Venusians you came in here with the clap.

Jimmy sewed and the nurse poured a little more.

---Have you thought of hanging out with Plutonians? Jimmy asked.

Yet more incoherent mumblings issued from the drunk and yet more nodding and sewing from Jimmy, punctuated with a bemused shake of his head as he finished.

---Give him a shot and let him lie down for thirty minutes then ship him off to his next planet.

---Is he going to Pluto? I asked.

---He doesn't like cold weather. He's going to look for UFOs from Mercury.

---Good plan. By the way, hello.

The drunk smiled up at me. I thought I saw a tooth in his mouth, but I wasn't sure. I hoped his next visit was to a planet of dentists. He wandered off with the nurse and I stuck out my hand to Jimmy.

---Let me scrub first. You wouldn't want the diseases he's got.

He went to a sink to scrub and then poured a foul-smelling liquid over his hands, dried them and turned to me.

---Coffee?

Charity Hospital is a utilitarian place, once you get past the art deco exterior and entrances. It was built to inspire from the outside and to serve on the inside. The halls, wards, and rooms are lined with six feet of white tiles with white plaster walls above that and an equally bland ceiling overhead. The nursing stations are frequent but Spartan, the rooms are arranged for maximum capacity.

With that in mind, the cafeteria was no surprise. The noise reverberated off the white tiles, bounced off the plain white walls and echoed down from the ceiling above. Since it was constructed when the word constructed still had meaning as opposed to the jerry-built objects we throw up today, those walls and ceilings were of solid steel and masonry. The cafeteria was loud. That was OK. We were safer talking in the middle of that maelstrom than in any hideaway with spy holes and listening devices.

---You want me to do what? Jimmy asked stirring his coffee.

---Look at an autopsy report.

---Where did this come from?

---You don't want to know.

---Why am I doing this?

---You don't want to know.

---Is this legal?

He paused briefly.

---I don't want to know.

I handed him the manila folder over the table. Like I said, openness was a better safeguard than an elaborate attempt at cleverness.

---Have you read this?

---No.

---Why not?

---It's my father's.

He grunted. I know all the arguments about the utility of autopsies and the benefit to the medical profession and future patients, blah-blah-blah. If you know what an autopsy is, you will understand why you don't want to see one performed on someone you love.

---Are there pictures?

---Why do you think I haven't opened the envelope?

---Give me a minute.

He stirred his coffee with his left hand while his right hand sifted through the papers. I made a detailed study of the acoustic tiles overhead so that my eyes would not accidentally see something they did not want to see.

It takes time to count the number of tiles in the ceiling of a room as large as the cafeteria. That I was reduced to counting the number of holes in the tiles in the ceiling, gives you an idea as to how thoroughly Jimmy read the report.

Around the time I decided that I was going to need traction to correct the crick in my neck from counting tiles, Jimmy reshuffled the papers and returned them to the envelope. His eyes didn't find mine as he picked up his cup.

---My coffee's cold.

---That's because you stirred it for forty minutes and never sipped it once.

---I can't talk with cold coffee.

---I'll get you a fresh cup.

---I'll get it.

He scurried off to the serving line. Jimmy always scurried, partly because he was short, and partly because he was always in a hurry.

Jimmy was slow to come back, but I expected that. He wanted the time to think more than he wanted coffee and I wasn't about to rush him. Eventually, he came back and started stirring his coffee again. I reached over to stop his hand.

---I am not going to sit here while you spend the day going back and forth for fresh coffee because you chilled your cup with breeze from stirring.

---What was the conclusion on your father?

---Accidental death.

---From?

---A fractured skull possibly sustained in a fall. There was evidence that he had fallen and the detectives added two and two.

---Did they come up with six?

I got very still.

---Meaning?

---I've made my diagnosis.

I got very still and worked to swallow the gravel in my throat.

---Which is?

Black horn-rimmed glasses can be very intimidating. They punctuate the face and provide a platform for light to refract off them, giving the wearer the look of a magus.

---The patient died from a fractured skull which could have resulted from an accidental fall.

It wasn't what I expected or maybe it wasn't what I was hoping. The desire to avenge a loss or a wrong is a powerful emotion. I wanted someone to pay for my father's death. Maybe I was just going to have to deal with it. That was disappointing.

---They were right?

He actually swallowed some coffee.

---You always were hasty.

---Give.

---The injury had to have been inflicted at least six weeks previously, judging from the size of the hematoma.

---That's crazy. Would he have been in pain?

---Yes. Would your dad have consulted a doctor?

---Hell, yes.

---So?

I closed my eyes to think. I always close my eyes to think. It was a very bad habit. But, in the darkness, sometimes light comes.

---The report can't be on him. It's a fake.

The words were out of my mouth before I realized what I was saying. Then, I did. I looked across the table at Jimmy. The young cop's suspicions and my gut just might be on to something. If that was the case, my reason for being in town just got a whole lot more serious. I had to hear myself say it again.

---It's a fake.

Across the table, Jimmy gently patted his hands together in applause.

---Your schooling was not a total waste after all, grasshopper, he said.

---If it's a fake, there's a cover up.

---And if there's a cover up?

---There's something that needs to be covered.

We both sat in our own thoughts. Mine were a little jumbled. Jimmy just looked wise. Jimmy always looked wise. Jimmy was wise. Or else he had that inscrutable thing down pat. I looked across at him

---What are you into? he asked.

---I'm not sure yet, I said.

---Will it put customers in my ER?

---Possibly.

---Well, you always were good for business.

---I'm an actor. As I keep having to remind people.

---So was John Wilkes Booth.

---I'm no assassin.

---He didn't think he was, either. He saw himself as an avenging angel.

He had me there and he knew it.

---Your coffee's getting cold, I said.

He looked down at the cup and pushed it across the table. He shrugged.

---That's all right. I don't like coffee anyway.

I had a lot on my mind when I left the hospital. Ramirez and Jimmy, plus my midnight dance at Parasol's had given me a lot of food for thought.

CHAPTER TEN

There was nothing to be gained by putting it off, so I headed over to the fire station near Charity Hospital. I didn't know if BroBoo was on shift, but what I needed could be gotten whether he was there or not. In fact, it might be easier if he were not. He could be testy at times.

When I walked the short two blocks from the hospital to the firehouse, I could see a knot of men in serious discussion in front of that big door the engine springs out of like a shot if the bell rings. It wasn't football season, and their tone was too subdued to be talking about sex, so I had a pretty good idea that the menu for the evening was under discussion. I was too late for lunch, but if I was able to stretch it out, I could still be there for dinner.

I couldn't believe my luck. I would have input. With input came sharing the chore of preparing the meal, but that was all right. I love to watch artists at work.

Now, there are a lot of good places to eat in New Orleans, and there are more than a few great places to eat in New Orleans, then there are those places that soar into the stratosphere, and a firehouse meal was one of them. As far as I knew, the ability to cook was not a part of the application or training process, but I never ate a firehouse meal that wouldn't bring tears to your eyes.

Possibly it had to do with the fact that, once a firefighter cleaned his equipment and trained, there was damn little to do until the times you ran into a fire to save something or someone who possibly didn't deserve to be saved. Firefighters never saw it that way. Think of it a minute: every sorry sumbitch in the world runs *out* of a fire on the very simple grounds that to stay in one will get your ass fried to the point that there may not be anything recognizable left to bury. A firefighter runs *into* a fire. Can you explain that? I can't. Except maybe the fact that they were issued more equipment in their jockey shorts than the public has a right to expect.

Anyway, while you are sitting around waiting to get your ass fried for a ridiculously small salary, there is little to do except watch television and cook. Since the opportunities you have to eat a really good meal are strictly limited by the chancy odds of the life you have chosen, the desire to eat well is strong. As the city budget barely pays your salary, cooks are not one of the perks of life in a firehouse. You fend for yourself. Necessity being a mother, fire fighters learn to cook.

The only thing to compare with the process of preparing a firehouse meal is the fish market at Pike's Place in Seattle, only firefighters are not tossing huge fish but meat, vegetables, pots, pans, and knives. It's amazing that a meal gets cooked without death or serious injury, but, like I said, they're artists. And damn good cooks. I wasn't there for a meal, of course, but for information, of course. On the other hand, it would be impolite to refuse an invitation. And even more impolite for them not to issue one. It worked.

After eating, burping, and small talk, it was time for the purpose of my visit which was only partly about eating, burping, and small talk. I edged up to the captain and cleverly probed for information.

---Dad hung around here after he retired?

---Some. Other firehouses, too.

---To do what?

---Talking.

---Talking about?

---This and that.

It's the water. The Mississippi is so filled with silt it slows down the neural pathways from brain to mouth.

---You been hanging with Red John?

BroBoo put a stop to the existential conversation by leading us out to the garage where it was quiet and there was no burping.

---Ever since Bubber died, Dad was a man with a mission.

---Which was?

---How Bubber died.

---You gonna tell me?

BroBoo looked at the Captain who nodded.

---I'm gonna show you.

It was nearly dusk, and the city was lit by that watery blue light that paints New Orleans evenings from a palette few cities can offer. The darkness was rising from the streets and gutters to flow over the banquettes and up the front of houses where the setting sun picked out the Victorian gingerbread of the shotguns with the same delicate shading it accorded the mansions of the Garden District. We took a left to head toward the river.

I looked forward to seeing the neighborhood I had grown up in, with all the crowded life and color that comes from people of mixed ancestry, races, and origins butting cheek and jowl on a daily basis. It always soothed my soul. I hunched a little in the seat and craned forward to let my eyes feast on the cool drink of water that memory supplies and got hit with a shot of scalding steam.

---What the hell happened? I asked.

BroBoo turned the wheel to cruise the desert of what had once been streets full of people and life and that funky brew of food and music that defines the city. It was a wasteland

---Urban renewal. There's gonna be a big new complex here with shops and hotels and condos and casinos.

---A rake off paradise.

---To say nothing of the hookers and junkies.

--- Who signed off on this canker sore?

---Concerned city fathers and leaders.

---So, people were scooping up bribes.

--- With both hands.

---What's this got to do with Bubber?

---He liked his house. Didn't want to move. So, he got moved.

---I was told that was an accident.

---Yeah. Like Bigfoot, Santa, and fairies.

Now that was going too far. When you impugn fairies, you're talking about some of my best friends.

---Your dad just wanted to make sure. Then he died.

---I want to be sure about some things, too.

BroBoo looked at his Captain, then over his shoulder at me with a grin.

---Insurance paid up?

Like a rotted stump of a tooth in a gaping, decayed mouth, one old building stood among the ruin. Why it had escaped the wrecking ball was a mystery. It offered no architectural merit and few signs of life.

---What's that?

---Old warehouse. A politician uses it as his headquarters

---For what? The city rats?

---Truer than you know. He's the head rat.

---What's his name?

---Duplantis. Judge Duplantis, but the only thing he judges is the weight of your wallet or whether a dolly'll raise her legs to get a favor.

A car cut around the corner directly into our path and BroBoo had to swing the wheel sharply left and right to avoid him which he did, but it sent us into a spin which had us heading for a fire hydrant which would have done little for the grillwork. He cut in the direction of the skid and we straightened out to stop inches away from the silver stand.

---Nice driving.

---Kill that sonvabitch if I could.

---Where'd he go?

---Pulled into the warehouse. Probably one of the pimps that works for that sorry bag of horse dung.

Actually, he didn't say "dung." He said a good deal more, but it would be repetitious, so I'll skip over it. Our conversation and our drive were pretty well over, so we headed back to the firehouse.

It wasn't that far from the firehouse to the Public Library at the edge of the Civic Center so I walked. I wanted to see what the newspapers had to say about that series of unfortunate incidents clustered in that area by the docks that used to be a nice working-class neighborhood.

Almost buried on an inside page was a tiny item that my eye caught by accident. It was about some judge who was suggesting that the area, since it was so derelict, be put to a use that would benefit the public. He suggested building a new center to attract conventions to the city to make up for the oil bust. I'm sure it was a fine idea, if you hadn't lived there and loved the lifestyle the neighborhood provided. Then that actor's mind I own, the one that sees subtext everywhere, started to work and I wondered if all those unfortunate incidents had been unfortunate or planned.

As I closed out the microfilm file, I had a sudden thought that I wanted to confirm, so I turned back to Bubber's death notice. My pack rat memory was right. If I could put two and two together and get six, I wondered if my father, who was a whole lot smarter than I will ever be, had done the same arithmetic and come up with four. That'd be like him. It would also be like him to investigate. And it would be very like him to take action, if he thought action was required. But did someone take action on him before he could drop the nickel? That was my question to answer.

I left the library in a very thoughtful mood.

The library and my calls on Ramirez and Jimmy, and my gig as Fred Astaire outside Parasol's, gave me plenty to think about. As I chewed on it, I headed to Space's place. It might be a little premature, but I needed comfort, so I decided to get something to wrap my hand around in an emergency.

Space didn't even look up when I came in. He had his head in the innards of something electronic and would seem to anyone who didn't know him to be lost to the world.

I went to the pocket at the far middle of the table and stuck my hand inside. For the pocket of a pool table, it was very deep. Nested at the bottom was an oily cloth that had a lot of weight to it for an oily cloth. I laid it on the green baize top of the table.

---You had it out.

---Old boy scout. Always prepared.

I spread it on the table. The blued metal looked dull in the overhead light.

I got something cold for us to drink and we sat on the patio. I filled him in on what little I had learned. I didn't tell him about Bryna. I always hated it when he rolled his eyes that way. We both knew my history with meaningful relationships. Chickens had a better chance at Popeye's than I did with most of the women I ever cared for.

As he drained his bottle, I asked the question, which was the second reason I came here.

---If you were me, what would you do next?

---What you doin'?

---Poking.

---Where you think you got?

---Not sure. I got jumped the other night.

---Was it a mugging?

---Didn't take anything. So I guess I'm getting somebody's attention.

---Why don't you poke some more?

---Why?

---Why not?

That sounded a lot like marching orders, so I started back to pick up the oily cloth.

---Leave the package.

I stopped. He was looking at me with his patented Sapient Look #3.

---Why?

---One mugging? C'mon. No real need for it yet, is there?

---Maybe not.

---Come back when there is.

He gave a nod and I headed out, leaving him to another excruciatingly small piece of electronics. Space kept tinkering. So did I.

CHAPTER ELEVEN

Rehearsal was in full swing so I didn't bother Don. I headed backstage to look for my favorite stage manager. The ASM told me she was covering a role in the show and was busy with a costume change at the moment. I slid between two flats so I could see the stage. I saw a whole lot more. The stage lighting was blue. Her skin was white.

She was changing in a little cubby formed by two flats on the other side of the stage. No one was around and I suppose she figured she was safe from prying eyes. She was almost right. Knowing I shouldn't look, I looked. I ought to be ashamed.

Her body flowed in a smooth ski slope my fingers longed to schuss. One hip faced forward, the light from a baby spot just illuminating the top band of her bikini bottom. It was lavender. The rest of her was shadowed. I was glad. I would have died had I seen more and I wanted to live until I had my fill of her, and that would make me a very old man, indeed.

She was a whole series of triangles set one on top the other in an arrangement that Picasso would have admired. Her small, triangular head tipped back, a sharp, but delicate, nose searched the air above her. Her bosom jutted forward in a pleasing angle against the blackness to complete the composition. The blue tint of the lights on her fair skin gave her an otherworldly glow and the backlight haloed her hair. Standing there, she was a cross between an angel and a wild woodland sprite. The lights gave her an angelic glow, and the shadows cut her face into Pan-like angles.

Apparently, she was well into the change, having gotten out of one costume and about to get into a backless dress that required her to reach behind to unsnap her brassiere. Two pert little fellows popped out, as firm and proud without any assistance as with a bra.

It seemed like a long time since I had seen the guys. This time I saw them without a cloaking veil of tears. I was glad I was across the stage from her. The temptation to cradle them like new-born kittens would have been too much.

She slid into the dress and zipped it up. You could tell she was a stage manager, because she took the time to hang up the discarded costume before she turned for her entrance. Some actress types would have left the costume on the floor.

I tiptoed out. She couldn't hit me from where she was, but I didn't want her to know I had seen her. This moment was going to be mine, to take out on bad, lonely nights when the world seemed rotten. Not so, I would say. I once saw something wonderful.

I found a place in a back corner of the lobby. I wasn't hugging the image to my chest like some sex addict. I had a feeling of such peace that I wanted to just sit and let my mind turn over like a film projector spooling out a newsreel. I was going to some Zen place where I could hold that picture in my mind and repeat her name to myself so the world would slip away and I would see eternity with great clarity.

I was staring at the artwork near the drink machine, sitting on the lobby's cold tile floor with my back against the brick wall and my chin resting on my knees when she came out to lock up.

She stopped in the act of switching off the hall light.

---What are you doing here in the dark?

---Trying to decide. Would you mind if I was to fall in love with you?

She was silhouetted against the hall light so I couldn't read her face, but her head canted at an angle that told me the wheels were turning under that beautiful blonde hair.

---Pathetic line. Let's go for a drink.

Well, the chance to get a girl drunk so you can work your wicked way on her is as standard a theatrical plot as you could want, and one I'd played often. Onstage. What do you think I am? OK. A couple of times offstage.

I didn't have to twirl my mustache, though. As it turns out, a drink can be any form of liquid. In Bryna's case, it didn't mean alcohol. That being the case, we ended up in a little place across Esplanade Avenue from the Quarter.

I would not expect to see the food pyramid displayed on the wall of a French Quarter restaurant, but this was the Marigny. Also, a restaurant did not normally, in my experience, sell spices. There were rows of them and they were a little intimidating. I had seldom seen that amount of lettuce outside of a rabbit hutch.

Carping aside, it wasn't a bad little place. It was small, and quiet, and neat. The floor was cement. The walls were brick, and the music was nothing I had ever heard before, but it was soothing. Since they didn't serve alcohol, we had to decide on a drink from an aggressively healthy menu.

It is apparently possible to make tea out of things you would never think it possible to make tea out of. I chose passionflower. When it came, I was a little disappointed. The name was misleading.

---Not what you expected?

---Not where I would expect to go for an after- rehearsal drink.

---I don't drink. At least, I don't drink often.

---I don't either. It got to be a problem so I had to taper off to practically nothing. So, I drink little and seldom.

She fiddled with the little plastic flower next to the candle.

---It's a health thing. I sometimes drink wine.

---On special occasions?

---You might say that.

She took a breath, cleared her throat, and looked at the wall over my head.

---Mostly on, let's say, 'romantic' occasions to help me relax. I can be a little uptight.

---I see.

---No, you won't see. Don't get your hopes up.

I gave it a beat and asked, ---Tell me again what you ordered?

---Carrot juice.

---Damn.

She gave me that half turn of the head and the look upward from under her eyebrows. She seemed amused so I went with it.

---Does this mean we're not going to have 'romance?'

It was a throwaway, but she stopped to consider it like it was a question that needed an answer.

---I'm thinking about it. But not tonight.

Her eyes glittered in the candlelight like opals. I nearly

embarrassed myself on the spot.

The drinks came and she sipped at her carrot colada. I tried the passionflower tea. It was better than I expected, but not as passionate as one could wish.

---It wouldn't be a good idea to go around saying you fell in love with me.

---If I fell in love with you and don't tell anyone, would that be OK?

She got very quiet and it wasn't a good quiet.

---I'm not sure. You come on strong

I got the definite feeling not to go there. Just when I was casting about for a change of subject, she did it for me. She may have been as anxious as I was to get on safer ground.

---What were you really doing sitting in the dark?

Searching for passion, I sipped at my cup again and decided to load my tea up with sugar. Brown sugar, unprocessed, of course. I took my time stirring and didn't look at her. When I was ready and I thought the temperature might be a little cooler, I tried to frame my thoughts for her in a way that didn't give away too much.

---My father died.

---I know. I'm sorry.

---So am I.

---It happens, you know.

---I just have the feeling that he was helped on his way to that crown of glory.

---What makes you think that?

---Instinct.

---That's why you're poking your nose all over town? Instinct?

---My brain lies to me.

---Your instinct ?

---Never.

We sat quietly. I finished my tea. Most of it. She finished her juice. All of it. Then we walked into the night.

It was like walking in a protective pod to be with her. Mind, heart, and spirit slowed. Testosterone didn't, of course, but I told you I was an actor.

---What has your instinct told you lately?

---Two things.

---Yes?

---The first was that I need to be sure my father died because it was his time.

---The other?

---That I would like to spend the rest of my life making love to you.

She froze in the dark, and then started walking rapidly away. I had to hurry to catch up and, at that, nearly had to run. There was an icy chill in the air that had nothing to do with weather. I knew what the forecast was, so I didn't say a word. Eventually she slowed and we were able to walk at a pace that didn't require a defibrillator.

We were heading back to the theatre through the Quarter. I reached over to take her hand as we walked, but she slid out of my grip and folded her arms across her chest.

---Why do you want to hold my hand?

---Actually, I wanted to put my hand on your be-hind except I've been slapped by you before.

---Cute. Chaussier, you're a pervert.

How unkind. She just didn't know the depths of my soul. Or maybe she did. I never thought she was stupid.

It was pleasant walking with her. It would have been more pleasant holding hands, or, even better, her derrière. You can't have everything. I, of course, would continue to try for as much as I could get. I'm a man. And you know what bastards *we* are.

We were passing through a dark section and I thought I picked up the sound of feet behind us. It was always possible that I was being paranoid, but, like they say, "it's never paranoia when they really are out to get you."

I was quiet so she looked at me sideways out the corner of her eye. I hated it when she did that. It turned my knees to jelly and I might be going to need my knees in a minute.

---Are you sulking? she asked.

---It's just nice here in the dark with you.

---I don't believe it. You're upset because I wouldn't let you hold my hand.

---Nonsense. Let's just enjoy the dark.

We walked in silence for a few seconds. There were definitely footsteps behind us. Keeping pace, maybe closing in a little, but footsteps there.

---Don't read too much into this, but if I let you put your hand on my ...rear, would you feel better?

Now? How could I possibly say 'yes,' when we could be attacked at any minute? The footsteps seemed awfully close.

---Yes, I said.

---Pervert.

I thought she was bluffing. I didn't mind. It gave me time to think. Except what I was thinking of was my hand on her behind.

The footsteps sounded closer. I slowed my pace a little. If they were going to catch up to us, they were going to do it on my terms. I slowed more. Definitely. The footsteps were closer. It was funny. They had to know that I knew they were there. It was possible they didn't care I knew they were there.

There was a dark patch ahead. That's where I would make my move. I had better get the girl out of the way. I reached for Bryna's elbow. She stopped.

---OK, she said.

---What?

---I don't know why, but...you can put your hand ...there.... Just for a minute.

This was insane. I didn't have time for this. We could be in a street fight at any minute. She stopped in the shadow and turned to me.

---Well?

She was great: lovely, round and soft, yet firm enough to provide a resting place for your hands. Fairness required that I, at the very least, express my appreciation with a gentle squeeze, so I did. That turned out to be a mistake, because one squeeze was never going to be enough. I pulled her to me as hard as I could, really delightful girl parts pressing against what I hoped she would find interesting boy parts. For a moment, I entertained hopes. Unhappily, just then, the footsteps caught up to us.

I backed her away and shrugged my shoulders to loosen them. For someone who had no interest in being interrupted, I was ready. Anywhere but in New Orleans, the words that floated to us from the night would be thought a non-sequitur.

---Hey, are you Catholic?

---Do you swallow, honey?

Crap, a couple of youth exercising their First Amendment right. Was I supposed to faint? Did I really look like a suburban mark who would blush and run?

As they passed with smirks on their faces, I stretched out to leg whip the first one. He wasn't expecting it and went forward face first. His partner stopped short, so I continued my leg around and caught him between the legs. They both made funny sounds as they went down. I swung Bryna to the rear to be a barrier if they wanted to contest the issue.

They didn't. They got to their feet, suggested I perform a physical impossibility and took off down the street. I turned to a wide-eyed Bryna.

---Are you insane? she asked.

---They startled me, I said. ---I didn't intend to hurt them.

---You could have fooled me.

I watched as the two guys turned the corner, flipping the happy motoring salute as they went.

---You can let go of me, now.

I turned to look at her. Her face looked stern, but her eyes were smiling.

Apparently, I'd kept my hand on her cute butt the whole time. I was better than I thought I was.

---Do I have to?

She shook her head at me pityingly.

---Yes, you do.

---If I'd known they were going to mess up my best shot this way, I would have hit them harder.

She removed my hand and gave me a glance from the corner of

her golden eyes.

---Who said it was your best shot? and started down the street.

It rooted me to the spot. Then, she did that look over her shoulder again. I was getting to hate that look. It always got my hopes up. On the other hand, it was better than getting my face slapped. I caught up to her. On the chance her offer was still good, I put my hand on her waist and let it slide south. She looked straight ahead, but I knew she was smiling.

---Keep your hands to yourself.

---Yes, sir, I said.

We walked along for a few minutes. I could see her brow furrowing. I waited.

---What was that about?

---I like touching your booty.

---Not that. Your karate display.

--- I got jumped the other night.

---Why?

---I don't know.

Our footsteps were loud in a silence that wasn't quite as comfortable as it had been.

---You seemed awfully good at that fighting thing. Where'd you learn it?

--- All actors learn stage combat.

---All right. Don't tell me.

She huffed down the block. I ran to catch up. I took her elbow and turned her to me. She didn't meet my eyes.

---I'm sorry. I was jumped the other night and I don't know why. It may be nothing more than being in the wrong place at the wrong time or, it may have been deliberate. When I heard those guys behind us, I took precautions.

---Why are you so good at it? And don't give me that stage combat crap again.

---I was trained to be good at it.

---Can I ask where?

Now that was a tough one. I couldn't answer, but I didn't want to shut her out.

---If I told you, I'd have to kill you.

She almost flared back, but we did that silent walk thing again and this one was even less comfortable.

---So, you killed people.

---As a matter of fact, no.

---I thought you were trained for it.

---I was *in training* for it.

---So?

---As it turned out, I had scruples. So, I became an actor instead.

---I never heard of that before.

---An attacker who doesn't attack?

---No. An actor with scruples.

She was smiling, so it felt right to slip my arm around her waist to draw her closer. She looked at me a long moment.

---Why would someone attack you?

---If I knew that, I'd be closer to answering the question that brought me home.

---And that is?

---Why is my father dead?

---People die.

I nodded. I knew that, but I couldn't say more

---As long as it's in their own time, OK.

---You think it wasn't?

---I don't know. I don't like not knowing.

---Do you have to know everything?

---Most things.

---What else do you need to know?

---There is one thing. I was wondering if you could help me find out.

She stopped and turned to me. My face was shadowed, but I could see every bit of hers.

Looking at me a long time, I supposed she was trying to pierce the darkness of the night, or the darkness of my heart. I could tell her a lot about both.

After a long time, her face got very soft and she spoke

deliberately.

    ---I'll help you. If I can. What do you want to find out?

    ---Do you snore?

For a second she froze, then her face got red at the implied situation she'd be in. Next her eyes narrowed because she knew she'd been had. She wanted to laugh but wouldn't. She wanted to fly off the handle, except she didn't, and that was good news. Finally, she hit me. I expected her to, but it was more or less a love tap so it was more than okay.

    ---You are impossible and a chauvinist pig.

I do a good innocent rube. I've played Tony Lumpkin.

    ---Is that a "no?"

    ---That means you'll never find out.

It *wasn't* a "no" and that was potentially very good news so I kept up the teasing.

    ---Did you ever read <u>The Count of Monte Cristo</u>?

Got her of balance again. I was having a good day.

    ---I suppose this is going somewhere?

I didn't really mean anything by this. I was just riffing to extend the evening as long as I could, but she looked interested, and I liked having her interested in me.

    ---I was thinking of the last line of the book.

    ---Which is?

    ---"Wait and hope."

Her brow wrinkled and her eyes squinted and it was cute as hell.

    ---And your point is?

    ---Well, like Monte Cristo, I'll just wait and hope.

She was at the outer edge of curiosity and rage. But however the evening had gone, she would be thinking about me as she fell asleep, hopefully with a smile on her face.

    ---For what, for God's sake?

    --- To find out if you snore.

She hit me again. I expected she would.

    ---Does this mean I won't find out whether or not you snore?

    ---Figure it out yourself.

I hoped I had, but it was about as far as it was safe to push things just then. Since I was into quotations that night, I went with Scarlett O'Hara.

--- "Tomorrow is another day..."

I don't know if she recognized the line but I got the red blush and the narrowed eyes and her voice wasn't angry.

---It might be. But don't be too sure. I'm not what you think...

---Is it all right if I "wait and hope...?"

Her face was hard to read, but her body got soft.

---No harm in that, I guess...

I lifted her chin for a kiss that took some time because I was pretty sure tomorrow would come.

CHAPTER TWELVE

Don was up unusually early. For Don. When he came out of the bedroom, I was sitting on the couch with my feet on the coffee table reading and drinking coffee I had bought at the corner store along with the morning paper. I was also eating one of his English muffins and the orange marmalade with the kick to it that he always stocked.

I handed him a second coffee, black, no sugar that I brought for him. He took it with a monosyllabic grunt. I didn't expect anything other than monosyllabic grunts for some time. He was not a morning person.

He took a long pull on the coffee and headed to the kitchen to make a full pot. I never used his coffee maker. Brewing coffee was a religious ritual with him and who am I to profane another man's temple?

I was well into the sports page by the time he came out with muffin, OJ, marmalade pot and a huge mug of coffee. He sat in the bucket chair and disappeared behind the op-ed section. All I could see was the newspaper, the smoke rising from his cigarette, and an occasional hand reaching for the muffin or the mug. I raised my eyes from the sports page at a sound that wasn't a mumble.

---Have I reminded you recently how much you owe me?

---It might be faster if you just told me what you want.

--- I've lost both my male and female supporting players.

---That was careless.

---I want you to learn the part and open in four days.

---Is that all?

---You're the one person in town who could do it.

---This, I take it, is the con.

---Bryna is playing the other role.

---This, I take it, is the carrot.

---Do I need a stick?

A quick flash of Bryna in the blue light passed before my fevered eyes.

---No.

---I didn't think so.

He was quiet for a few minutes, and then cleared his throat. Don never cleared his throat and this was done in such a peremptory fashion that I almost expected what followed.

---You like her, right?

---Right.

---Don't play hit and run. Be good to her.

That was interesting. Don never intruded in anyone's personal life without invitation, and I never intruded in his without invitation. It made it possible for two prickly personalities to get along. I looked at him until he continued.

---She's a good person and she doesn't have an easy life.

---Is this something to do with her brother?

---You know about that?

---I only know there is an issue.

---She tell you?

---I have excellent antennae.

---If she didn't tell you, it's not for me to say anything. Just remember. She's a valuable person. Her life is complex.

---You mean complicated.

---My use of words is always precise, he said and left the room.

Even for a cryptic man, that was more than usually cryptic, but I had a script to master

Since I had read the play before, and seen a few rehearsals, I had a general idea of what was going on. He gave me a script and I read it with my body sprawled on the couch and my head hanging over the edge. It's not a comfortable way to read, but I always felt it helped me concentrate. Or I liked the rush I got from all the blood flowing to my head.

There were about thirty pages to learn. That was the bad part. I had a love scene with Bryna. That was the good part. I spent a few hours trying to commit the lines to memory. My mind wasn't wandering for a change. I wasn't thinking about what had brought me to town, at least it was a break from that. Although, I was wondering why Bryna was stage managing if she was good enough to step into the role. Why was she stage managing, anyway? She obviously had talent as a visual artist. Given some of the junk you saw in the Quarter, she could easily make a living at that.

She didn't strike me as being one of those stage- struck groupies who would clean commodes to be around the theatre, yet she obviously did the scut work and anything else that was called for. There was a story there and I needed to get it for three reasons: A. I am naturally curious about people, places, and things, B. I tend to really get into a person, place, or thing that I feel strongly about; and C. I was getting suspicious about everyone who crossed my path on my New Orleans sojourn.

Call it paranoia. I call it healthy caution. There are times when healthy caution enables you to keep breathing longer, and I was fond of breathing. Since making the acquaintance of a certain pair of golden eyes, I wanted to breathe a whole lot longer.

This was doing nothing to prepare me for my understudy shot, so I picked up the script again. Marc decided it was time for a post-prandial snooze, so he put his butt in my face. A sight less conducive to study it would be hard to imagine, so I took myself out the door and down the street.

It was a good thing the meal filled me, because even though I had taken the script to memorize lines, it was slow going. I persevered. The reward would be acting opposite Bryna. That ranked high on my "to do" list.

I maintain that you can tell volumes about a person by acting with them. With some actors, their eyes are focused on the unseen mirror of their egos, judging how each moment looks to the viewer. Others are terror-stricken, either searching for the next line, or questioning the universe that led them to that moment. Other actors have completely dead eyes.

A few actors let you into their souls. Their eyes connect with you, and you feed each other in a communion beyond words. That's when the magic happens. The actors who give you that are few, and are to be cherished. I hoped she was like that. I suspected she was. I would find out. If only I learned the damn lines.

I put a lot of cream and sugar in my coffee and turned to the script, resolved to block out everything and admit of no interruptions. Wrong.

I saw him coming to my table. I was getting better at finding people who were aiming themselves at me. There was nothing threatening about him. I thought for a second he might be a fan, which would be odd because I had few fans, and none I knew of in New Orleans.

He had on jeans and a gray sweatshirt which looked frayed but well cared for. His face was pale or maybe his jet-black hair and blue eyes made him seem that way. He was nervous but not jumpy. He didn't seem like a junkie in need of a fix or somebody who owed me money. I don't know who that could have been in any event. Maybe he *was* a fan. He had that pleading quality that you find in autograph seekers

---Jeff Chaussier?

I opted for fan, and gave him the delighted smile of someone who has been recognized on the street despite a cunning disguise.

---Yes. How are you?

He twitched and licked his lips, and I decided I was far off in my guesses. He was a panhandler. With a poor sense of marks.

---OK. Not so good. I need to talk to you.

While sorting that out, I decided to be gracious.

---Have a seat. I was just going over my lines. I'm an actor.

His eyes actually lit up and he swiveled into the chair almost eagerly.

---I know. I've seen you on stage.

Good. A fan. They're in short supply. I decided I could preen a little.

---I used to come to your plays when I was a little kid.

That tore it. No autograph for him. He went back to lip licking anyway.

---Somebody asked me to give you a message. Since I know who you were. Not a lot of people do.

He was *not* going to be fan club president. I'd black ball him.

---Look, could we go outside? This guy wants to talk to you and people make him nervous.

---What's he do?

---He's kind of an actor.

---And people make him nervous.?

---Just in a group. Not you.

His career would be limited. There aren't many shows you can perform to one person and make a living. OK. Another sidewalk *tete a' tete*. Somebody wanted to talk and I had come to New Orleans to listen.

The kid had a puppy dog harmless look and I was in search of information. Also, the sun was shining. Anyone jumping me on a sidewalk in sunshine was an incompetent. Of course, we could be going into an alley.

---I'm going to need at least a name before I go anywhere.

The kid bit his lip and looked at the tile floor. Decisions seemed hard for him.

---I guess it's OK. His name is Tommy. He spells it with an 'i' for professional reasons.

A smile creased my lips. There could only be so many Tommys "with an 'i' for professional reasons," even in New Orleans.

If it was him, I might learn something and, at this time of day, I would almost certainly be treated to a sight to see.

---For a few minutes. I have lines to learn.

He rose and I got up with him. He sat down. Looking around, he whispered, convict style, from the corner of his mouth.

---Not together.

Sliding out of his chair with elaborate nonchalance, he cocked his head.

--- Follow me out.

He was up and gone before I could ask what the hell. He was the world's poorest choice for an agent holding surreptitious meetings.

I watched him weave his way to the dark wood door with the frosted glass panels.

I couldn't see him once he left.

Tujacque's has tall French windows but they have white curtains gathered at the top and bottom so you only have a couple of slits for viewing. I decided to follow him. It was a good excuse not to study lines.

CHAPTER THIRTEEN

I saw the kid duck into an alley so I did, too. It probably wasn't wise, but wise left the building with Elvis. Besides, I wanted to hear what Tommy "with an 'i' for professional reasons" had to say. He wasn't there. I would have cursed the Fates for a wild goose chase and the fact that there was nothing left but to learn lines, but as I turned to leave a voice called my name. It was a whispery voice, obviously faked, but loud enough to be heard.

I searched the darker parts of the alley with a steady stare, though I stayed on the periphery where a quick hop and step would get me in the light and hustle of the Quarter. Not that police would be handy. They were keeping people from Iowa safe on Bourbon Street. I toured Iowa once. Nice people. Can't party.

There was no place in the alley to hide and I didn't think firearms would be used in that location. That didn't make it safe, and I wasn't foolish enough to think so, but it made it less dire.

---You got about thirty seconds to come out here or I find you and either kick your ass or rearrange your face.

A voice trilled, as much as a baritone can trill, which isn't much. That's why tenors get the arias.

--What, you can't do both?

The ugliest woman I ever saw stepped out of the shadows smoking the biggest, thickest, smelliest cigar there ever was.

----Tommy, are you trying to give me a heart attack?

---You have no heart.

He was wearing a cocktail dress and a blonde wig, but the effect was spoiled because he hadn't shaved and his five o'clock shadow was at about half past six.

---Why are you in drag at this hour anyway?

He flicked the ash off his cigar and inhaled enough smoke to cure bacon.

---Dress rehearsal for the new show at the Cupcake.

If you ever get a chance to catch Tommy's show at the Cupcake Cafe, don't miss it. Some of the most beautiful costumes and talented performers you'll ever see. When he goes in full costume, makeup and wig, Tommy really is attractive. They all are. By the way, a drag performer is not necessarily gay. Tommy's wife leads the band and his son works the lights. It's a family affair.

I once asked Tommy if his son was going to follow in his footsteps, but he sighed and said as much as he loved his son, he just didn't have the *métier*. I knew what he meant.

---Have a seat. I'm on break and the band leader is a beast to work for.

---I hope you don't tell her that.

---I don't. The woman would put arsenic in the pasta.

---Why'd you send the kid?

---A lady is never seen without her makeup. Besides the kid is a fan of yours.

---I know, 'from when he was a little kid.'

---He's a nice boy. Runs errands around the theatre. Wants to be an actor but the talent, *meh*.

There were a couple of crates against the wall and Tommy kicked them out. He settled on one, spreading his skirt so it didn't drag on the wet ground. I put a foot on the other and leaned against the wall. I trusted Tommy but...

---I think I'll stand.

---Well, you're not gone stupid even if you're stupidly going around asking stupid questions that will get you dead stupid or dumb stupid with a Sicilian necktie.

---Wouldn't you?

Ash got flicked and smoke inhaled and expelled.

---Do you have anything to go on?

---Besides a dead father?

He reached to tug my arm, and I had to sit or get pulled over. Having seen the state of the ground, I didn't want it kissing my face, so I sat.

--Just friends here.

---Just friends.

He leaned against the wall and started to talk. I followed him, but I kept wondering if he was getting the back of the dress dirty. If he was, Dolores would brain him with a trombone. She designed the costumes too.

There was no proof my dad was killed, but it was a more or less open secret that he was going around rattling cages. That was unsurprising, if he suspected Bubber had been helped off the mortal coil before his time. My dad had a strong sense of justice, and even stronger loyalty to those he gave his affection to. In that, we were alike. He wasn't a passive man, though. He acted on his beliefs.

Bubber could have been an accident or landlord neglect. Then, too, somebody was buying and razing the old neighborhood. Dad would be offended by both. There are people who would be offended that he was even asking questions. That would offend my dad. There was a lot of offense going around.

Maybe there was nothing to all of it. Except that I was being followed. Or was I? I was an actor and given to drama. My brief exposure to the line of work I had so abysmally failed at gave me a bent toward conspiracy theories. Maybe it was just muggers. It could have nothing to do with me at all. There was still that black car that kept turning up. I think Tommy had decided that there was nothing suspicious about my dad's passing except that he went too soon. We all do. Well maybe not Hitler. Or mimes.

I heard him out and he left because his wife would brain him if he was late returning from break. When you think about it, it's not surprising he made his living in a dress, because his wife definitely wore the pants in his house. I stretched out my legs and leaned against the wall, my eyes on the patch of sky overhead.

I didn't have enough to go on, but Tommy hadn't come up with a good reason to stop. There were other people to see, and other thoughts to be thunk.

Before I did much of anything else, I might need to pay Space a quick return visit. He still had that good friend of mine at his house and I thought I maybe it was time I should start carrying him with me. Actually, Space had more than one friend, but I was thinking of a small Italian number that wouldn't call too much attention to its presence, but would be a friend in need. It might be premature, but I needed comfort. I decided to get something to wrap my hand around in an emergency.

Space didn't even look up when I came in. He had his head in the innards of something electronic and would seem to anyone who didn't know him to be lost to the world. I knew better, so I wasn't surprised at all when he raised one arm and pointed to the pool table without removing his eyes from his project.

I went to the pocket at the far middle of the table that was very deep and stuck my hand inside. The oily cloth that had a lot of weight to it for an oily cloth still nested at the bottom.

I hefted it in my hand. It was small, but I wasn't looking for a blunderbuss. I hated the damn things anyway and never liked the idea of using one. I laid it on the green baize top of the table.

---Didn't expect you quite this soon.

---I'm getting mugged by people who don't take anything.

---How many times?

---Twice. Time for the package?

He made a final adjustment to what he was working on while I watched.

---Time. Get something cold for us to drink.

We sat on the patio. We didn't say much, but we never did. I just liked to wrap myself in his presence. It was good to know that there was someone who would always be there. I was lucky. I had several someones. I was probably going to need them.

I was feeling better about things. I felt good enough to do something important. Like go to the theatre to rehearse.

CHAPTER FOURTEEN

When I walked into the dressing room after rehearsal, Bryna was brushing her teeth. It had been a damn fine rehearsal and my question was answered. Bryna was a giving actor. When you looked at her on stage, she looked back at you. I mean she looked. None of this: is my lipstick smeared; or what is my next line; or what shall I have to eat after the show.

She saw me in the mirror and raised one finger to wait as she continued brushing. I was more than happy to wait. I didn't know if brushing was a full body exercise for everyone, but it was for her. First, she moved in a swaying hula dance that made me think of moonlight and sea breezes. Her eyes rose to mine in the mirror and the brushing seemed to become more Latin, causing everything to move in many directions at once. I was being treated to a full dance revue, and I had the best seat in the house. I was all in favor of proper dental hygiene, so I made no objection. Cleanliness is next to lust.

I could see from the way her eyes smiled at me in the mirror while she dried her lips and hands that she knew where my eyes had been. I only hoped she didn't know where my mind had been, but she probably did. I had prepared a number of extremely witty things to say that would awe her with my brilliance. I never got to say them, because she came straight into my arms and planted her lips smack on mine. That is so much better than witty remarks. It is hard to describe how much better that is than witty remarks.

That may have been the best kiss of my life. It was a kiss that took all your attention and kept your total interest. She didn't just plant lips on yours or, even worse, wash your tonsils. Instead her lips went to mine and roved around, exploring the new terrain, politely introducing themselves, and inviting me to explore in turn. It was like being devoured by an animal with tiny lips so the devouring lasted forever. I couldn't think of a better way to go.

When it ended, I couldn't have said whether it took sixty seconds or sixty years. I just knew that I had never been kissed before and this was something I could develop a serious addiction to. She finally stepped back from me and looked directly into my eyes.

---I thought I owed you a kiss. I was ugly to you last night.

---What would I get for an apology if you did something downright vile?

She smiled that slow smile, leaning in to continue the conversation. Since I was better prepared this time, I would like to think I improved on my first effort. I can't say that she did. How do you improve on perfection? I had to sit down at the end of the kiss. As I did, I took her with me. She sat on my lap, playing with the sides of my hair and running those amazing eyes over my face.

---Sorry I had to sit down, I said. ---My legs got rubbery.

Her eyes had a wicked golden gleam.

---That's the only part of you that's rubbery.

Fortunately, I am past blushing, but if I still could blush, I would have.

---A medical condition, I said, ---I'm thinking of having surgery to fix it.

She brought her lips to my ear.

---Don't you dare, she whispered.

I could see the two of us in the mirror. It looked really natural to have her sitting on my lap. Our shoulders were the same height in the glass and, even allowing for the fact that she was on my lap, it was a pretty good indication that, say, stretched out on a nice wide king size bed with cool silky sheets and a breeze blowing the curtains in the windows that just ruffled the hair on her forehead, and I was reclining on an elbow next to her drowning in her eyes while the tips of my fingers mapped every inch of her, we fit, if you know what I mean.

Her hands went into my shirt. I didn't want her to think she was being too forward, so I put my hands in her shirt. She was soft and cool to the touch, but there were fires within that scorched, even though I was far from the flame. The next few minutes are absolutely none of anyone's business.

Don't get prurient. Nobody got naked, and we certainly did not have sex. The dressing room quickie is such a cliché. Although honesty compels me to admit that both thoughts did occur to me. What do you expect? I'm a man. As to what she thought of me, you'll have to ask her. I hope she wasn't disappointed. Well, there was one thing. As we kissed, my hand got frisky and started marching up her thigh a little further than was gentlemanly. So, I pulled away.

---Sorry I said.

She grabbed my hand, replacing it with a light clasp.

---I don't mind. I should. But I don't.

---Well, it's possible I could fall in love with you, and I don't want to do anything I would later regret if that happened to be true.

She sat back and looked at my face for a long time.

---Stop saying, 'fall in love with me!' You barely know me.

---I am a very simple person. It could happen.

---Don't let it.

---You wouldn't like it?

---It's...not a good idea. At the very least, it's too much too soon.

---I'll try not to bring it up anytime soon.

---Please don't. It's...complicated...

There was a chill in the air, and I had put it there. I was sorry about that, but I was completely honest in what I said, and in what I thought I might be feeling.

---I need to change, she said.

---Can I stay in the room?

---Will you peek?

---I may try.

---Certainly not, she said, shaking her head.

---Can I watch from outside?

---Well, better not let me catch you.

She smiled that wonderful slow smile and turned to the alcove to change. I sat in the little anteroom and waited. I wondered if I should be offended that she thought I'd peek. I didn't. Let her catch me. Well, the mirror was right there. What do you expect?

I could have sat for hours watching the way she flowed, curves lengthening as she stretched and then coalescing into delightful convexities. Occasionally, I had to duck when her eyes passed my way. Since her lips were curved in a smile, I think she knew exactly what I was doing. And I don't think she was upset about it.

I had great plans for the evening, but I wasn't sure how to broach them. Especially since she came out wearing a man's suit with her blonde hair caught up under a fedora. She sat to put on a pair of man's dress shoes.

---Do you want to tell me anything about your cross-dressing addiction? I asked.

---It's protection.

---Against what? A bad review from GQ?

---Against your lust.

---What makes you think I won't attack you anyway? I may be gay.

---The evidence of the last twenty minutes is against that.

She had me there.

---I'm breaking in the shoes for the show. They're too little for the actor wearing them.

---And the suit?

---Same thing. Working the newness out.

I knew what she meant. You don't want an actor uncomfortable on stage. We're psychotic enough as it is.

We walked out the gate of the patio and started down the street. She came up to my shoulder with the hat on and took these funny little steps, perhaps because the shoes were hurting her feet. At any rate, we made a comical pair walking through the Quarter. At least, we did until I caught the sound of footsteps behind us.

This was getting to be a very aggravating occurrence. I tried to keep up a steady flow of conversation without losing track of the footfalls. Fortunately, she did most of the talking. She did a lot of laughing, too. It was really nice. Or, it would have been, if my focus hadn't been split.

This time there was no doubt. We were being stalked. They moved when we moved, stopped when we stopped, were invisible when I tried to catch a glimpse, and kept getting steadily closer. I was really tired of this and I was glad I hadn't let Space talk me into leaving the package behind.

We were in a residential area far from lights and tourists. The street ahead was dark and quiet. The footsteps got really close. They probably planned to take advantage of the darkness when we walked into it. I figured I'd better make my play. They were close, but not so close that I didn't have room to move.

I swiveled between two parked cars, jumped onto the hood, vaulted on top using my left hand, and slid down the back of the car to land right in front of them. I swung the side of the barrel of the gun across the head of the first one. He went down. When he did, I put the gun under the chin of the other as I pushed him against the wall. I pressed up on his chin as I cocked it. He lifted off his feet and his eyes were very glassy when he heard the action of the gun.

---Trick or treat, I said.

---Jesus Christ, the guy said.

---No. But I can send you to him.

---Jesus Christ, he said again.

He wasn't big on conversation. The guy on his knees made a move like he was trying to get to his feet, so I kicked him in the temple. Then I lifted my dance partner onto his toes by the simple device of pressing on his chin with the gun.

---Anything to add? I asked.

---Jesus Christ, he said yet again.

--- You say that one more time and my religious sensibilities might be so offended, I'll pull the trigger.

---Oh, shit, he said.

That provided variety, but no information. I grew testy.

---You want to tell me what you were up to?

---OK. OK. We thought you were faggots. We were going to roll you.

---Why?

---Kicks, man, just kicks. We didn't mean anything.

A passing cab threw enough light on his face that I could see he was a college age kid. He was very likely telling the truth. He was also very likely a jackass, but you can't shoot people for that. Well, you can, but it's frowned on.

---Do you think you and your buddy could get your happy asses down the street before my friend here gets frightened? I asked him.

---Yeah. Yeah.

---Get your buddy up and moving. I'm not sure how long it will take me to aim and fire, but I wouldn't take too much time, I said.

He hauled his friend up and they started down the block at a staggering lope, moving in a more or less straight line.

---And tell your friends, I called, ---us French Quarter faggots is touchy, dawling.

For a few seconds, I had forgotten Bryna. When I turned to her, her eyes were huge. She stared at me, pasty-faced. I reached to her. She took off down the block. I called to her, but she didn't stop. I didn't want to be undignified and run after her, but on the other hand, I might want to spend the rest of my life with her. I ran.

Her body was rigid when I caught up to her. She looked straight ahead and wouldn't acknowledge me. I figured I could wait her out. In the meantime, if she walked any faster, it would be an Olympic event. Around the time I was considering supplemental oxygen, she stopped. She was standing under a streetlamp. It may have been the light that made her face look pinched and angry, but I didn't think so.

I wasn't sure I was up to another hundred-yard dash, so I figured if I waited long enough, she'd have to talk to me. She stepped out of the light into total darkness. After a long time, she turned.

---Who are you?

Now, I was the one lit by the overhead streetlamp. Normally, I enjoy being in the limelight. This was one time I didn't.

---Someone who likes you. A lot...

We waited some more.

--- Why do you have a gun? she said.

---It's a prop.

---Bull.

---Well, it was a prop just now. I didn't fire it.

---Would you have?

I didn't want to answer that because the answer was "yes" and I was pretty sure it was not an answer that would please her. She removed her hat and held it before her like a shield, fingers playing nervously on the brim

---I know you would. I hate that I know...

I was glad that I didn't have to come out and say it, but I didn't think she received the news any better than she would have from me.

---You've used a gun before, haven't you?

Some images I never like to recall poked their heads into my mind. I took a second to ask them, politely, to leave. Bryna was ramrod straight in the dark and a much more accusing presence than anybody almost a foot shorter than me has any right to be. The most dangerous person I ever met in my life was under five feet tall. I watched him take three friends of mine apart. I think they dropped their guard because, despite all their training, for that one split second, they didn't think he was a threat. He was. That's why they no longer move so good.

---I almost did.

---Where?

---I can't tell you.

---You mean you won't tell me.

---A little of both.

She came into the light with her head down and placed the top of her head on my sternum so I couldn't see her eyes. We stood for another eternity. It was a night of pregnant pauses.

I tried to put my arms around her, but she stiffened, so I let my hands drop. She kept her head on my chest and her eyes on my shoes. When she started to speak, it was in a voice so low I could hardly hear her. She never got much louder, but I understood every word.

---I've had ... things in my life that aren't nice.

I put my arms around her again, and this time she let them stay there. I rested my chin on the top of her head.

---For whatever it may be worth, I would never hurt you.

She turned her head sideways and rested her cheek on my chest. I figured that was progress. When she let me run my hand up to the nape of her neck and massage the tautness I found there, that was even better progress. She brought my face to hers. I got the softest, gentlest kiss of my life and one that I hoped would last for the rest of my life. It didn't. She slid her hand down to mine and turned. I picked up her hat and we walked on.

The light cut across her face, accenting the pure white of her skin. I wasn't sure what her eyes were saying, but I thought I could still hope. What can I say? I'm a Pollyanna kind of guy.

We walked out of the streetlamp and into the night. It was quiet now, but not peaceful. I felt the tension in her but I was too smart, or too chicken, to bring it up so we walked for a long time, holding hands, brushing legs. After we walked for a while, her stride shortened and our thighs made more contact, and she held my hand tighter. Then, we slowed so much that, if we were cars, the honking behind us would have sounded like a thunderstorm. Her eyes were shadowed and the overhead lamp highlighted her fine bone structure.

She swallowed before and after she spoke and the Fates smiled. They practically giggled.

---Would you like to like to go to my apartment?

My head snapped to her. She looked at me from under her brows, a little girl asking to see Santa. Then she went on tiptoes, presenting more of herself to me, and I risked a kiss. That was a mistake, because it damn near killed me to separate my lips from hers.

---Yes.

Her arms tightened around my waist. Her voice got breathy, not sexy-breathy, more like she couldn't believe her own words.

--Would you like to lie in my bed?

I would say it was the humidity of the air in New Orleans that caused my breathing to get short, but that wouldn't be true. In for a penny, in for a pound. All she could do was slap me and she'd done that before.

---Would I be alone?

Her smile blossomed and her arms went around my waist as she leaned back to look at me. Her posture presented very important parts of her to very important parts of me, so I had no complaint. Especially since it caused a slow rolling movement that discouraged conversation.

I embraced her, lifting her off the ground and holding her to me by cupping her bum. She had a wonderful bum.

---Are you saying what I hope you're saying?

---I guess I'm saying I want to sleep with you.

Then she placed my hands so there could be no doubt. The next few minutes are not your business. When we broke, I was puzzled by something. Being an actor means being able to read faces. I had trouble understanding everything in hers. There was desire--thank heaven for little girls--and there was a hint of a smile, and there was a vulnerability that was very appealing.

---I'm such a fool...

All of that was very nice. I even understood the worry. She was her, and I was me, and we were an unlikely fit. I didn't understand the fear, though. It wasn't "am I making a mistake?" I could understand that. But I'd only seen fear like hers when I was in a place I can't mention, doing things I can't tell you about. The "I'm putting my life in danger" fear. I wanted to ask about it, but she wrapped a leg around my hips, then took in a breath. When she released it, I could barely hear her voice.

---This is such a bad idea.

I didn't know what that meant, so I didn't do or say anything, which is often a good idea. She tugged on my arm and we started down the street at a pretty good clip. It took a while before I could muster up a sentence.

---Why are we in such a hurry?

She stopped under a streetlight and opened my Christmas present for me.

---Because we're going to my apartment and we're going to make love for the rest of the night.

My face must have been a study because she laughed and leaned in.

---And maybe all tomorrow morning.

I'm a man of the world. I answered. Even if my voice was two octaves higher.

---O.K. by me, but why are we running?

She reached to give me a peck on the lips.

---This is a really bad idea. If I'm going to follow through on a really bad idea, I need to before... something changes my mind.

Then her lips parted and I made a mental note to put a little something extra in St. Jude's box at church.

We looked each other kind of bashfully, clasped hands, and started walking, sort of fast. She looked at me and I looked at her and we walked faster. By the time we got to her block we were running, blushing like twelve-year-olds. Maybe that was why I didn't notice the big dark whaleboat of a car idling in the street.

She stood in the moonlight as I removed her clothes. I took my time, because she was the best present I was ever going to get, and there was no reason to rush the unwrapping.

It takes a long time to undress someone properly, what with the little kisses and nibbles and licks. As her clothing slowly fell away, my eyes drank in a sight more beautiful than any I ever expected to see. The moonlight turned her into a silver goddess. The silver planes of her cheeks above a shadowed swan neck, its swoop hazy in shadow, coasted down to dark-tipped silver globes standing from the flat plain of her belly. I leaned to place a soft kiss on lips that opened to ignite a fire that burned deep inside us.

Once all those utterly unnecessary clothes were gone, she just stood. I picked her up, savoring her weight, her softness, and her warmth. I placed her gently on the bed, a snowy field of rolling hills and gentle declivities atop a field of lesser white. She saw me looking and her head turned to the side, then returned to me, fixing the moment for us both while we smiled at each other. When I lay beside her, I saw her eyes go to one of the paintings on her wall.

---This is such a bad idea.

I didn't think so, and I don't think she really felt that way. I was in the presence of someone very special and I told her so. By that time, we were in the position we had assumed in the same bed on another day, though, this time, without the barrier of clothing. We looked at each other and I think she remembered, because, she smiled, then I smiled. Her face got serious, then softened. We both kind of nodded and we shifted a little. After a slight adjustment of position, our smiles got broader. She played with the hair on my forehead and, as we became one, I barely heard her whisper.

--- This is absolutely the worst idea ever...

Then the sound of our breathing grew loud, and the room filled with words and little cries. I don't remember what we said. I know I said her name a lot and she said mine, and we told each other how much we liked each other, and how good what we were doing felt, and we said a lot about God or something. Then words disappeared and things got louder. Our breathing struggled to catch up to the pace of our movement and then our breath cut off. Our eyes met and she lowered her gaze. Then raising glowing eyes, we laughed together at the damp, heaving tangle we had become.

---Such a good bad idea, she said, smiling and playing with my hair.

I was afraid my weight atop her might be too much so I tried to get up, but she pulled me to her.

---Not yet. Stay.

Curls were plastered to her face and her gold eyes were feral when she looked up to me.

---I like feeling you atop me. I like it a lot.

We kissed and I rubbed her nose with mine. Then I rolled over so she was on top. She gave a happy laugh.

---This is so out of character,.. I can hardly believe I'm doing it.

---Staying up till dawn?

She laughed again and bit across my chest in little nips.

---Sleeping with someone I barely know.

---Well, you may not believe it, but it is for me, too.

She took my face in both hands and searched my eyes.

---Did you want *me*? Or am I just "tonight's girl?"

Well, I'm not great at that conversation, but I tried.

---No. Positively not. You're... I don't know, 'unique.' I've never met someone like you.

Her face may have turned a little pink, but I couldn't see because she drowned me in her special kiss then drew her head back to look at me again, a smile playing on her lips.

---I'm unique?

---Unique.

Her gold eyes glowed with a barely banked fire.

---You think I'm unique?

Her voice held the excited trill of a little girl.

---Then I need to be as unique as I can...

And she did. She certainly did. Now, I positively do not kiss and tell, but I'm not sure I could anyway. I only knew no one had ever made love to me so completely.

As we settled together, she bathed a love bite on me with her tongue:

—-I have never made love quite like that.

I don't know that anyone ever had. Ever could. I was awed. It was a total gift of self she presented me.

She raised a flushed face to mine.

--- I've never done that before.

---What?

Her face was glistening face as her hand passed through the wet strands of my hair.

---Be the one 'in charge.' I never am...

I lifted her chin.

---Why with me?

She lowered her face to my shoulder, giggling like a little girl. She didn't answer right away, but when she did, she looked puzzled.

---I don't know. I... had to. I just... I had to.

I watched the rising sun wash her shining white body with golden light. I didn't deserve to be lying there with her in my arms, but I wasn't about to trade it. Eyes lowered, face a fiery red, a bacchante and a shy little girl, her spider fingertips crawled down me.

---Of course, if you thought that was unique...

She looked at me with a wide smile and damp eyes.

---Could I, maybe, try to improve on it?

From the sound of her voice, I was in big trouble.

---I need a little time.

---I think I can help you with that.

Afterward, she lay with her head on my chest.

---Such a very good idea for being such a very bad idea.

The sun passed over her face to meet her eyes, slanted gold meeting rising gold, and a smile that was golden too. Our eyes met shyly. I know, not macho of me. But true.

---I wish....

---What?

The light in her eyes dimmed, replaced by a look I didn't understand then. She moved into my embrace, clinging like a limpet.

---Nothing. Just hold me.

I enclosed her in the circle of my arms. As we settled together, I inhaled the scent of her hair and savored the rise and fall of her breasts against my chest. I thought she might be crying. When I tipped her head back, her eyes were wet, but they were smiling, too.

---Such a very, very good idea... I won't forget tonight...

I didn't know what that meant. I didn't know a lot of things just then. I didn't know a big, black whaleboat of a car was idling outside her house.

Her eyes closed and I kissed the top of her hair. Feeling her warm body shiver against me, I pulled the covers over us as we fell asleep.

It was noon before we woke. There were chores to do. The clothes strewn around the bedroom had to be picked up. Breakfast needed to be fixed. I pitched right in. Since we didn't dress before we started, the chores took longer than they should. It was my fault. I was struck dumb by the exquisite flow of her body. It was like watching the world's best dancer. She seemed incapable of an ungraceful move. At first, she'd stop and blush and tell me to behave, but I think she got to like the total adoration coming from me.

Not that I didn't pull my weight. I was helpful. For instance, she didn't have to wash her back in the shower. I did that. I also rinsed her thoroughly, squeegeeing the water off with my bare hands. Drying was an issue. The towel worked well enough, but in the interest of thoroughness I insisted I had to check that she was really dry all over. It's a Boy Scout thing. At last, we were clean; but we didn't want to leave, even if we were due at rehearsal. At least I didn't. I think she agreed, because we spent a long time sprawled across the bed.

I could not get over the curve of her torso down to the swell of her hip, or the balance between the slight rise of her bosom and the gentle curve of her bottom. My head lay on the rise of round, velvet globes, lips exploring a white moonscape with feather touches. She seemed to twitch and titter a lot and finally stopped me with, what I hoped, was a satisfied chuckle.

---You know this may be the best bad idea ever.

I didn't want to seem too eager.

---Let's do it again tomorrow.

I expected a snappy rejoinder, but she played with my hair, her voice wistful.

---I don't deal in tomorrow...I...

When the time came to dress, we took turns dressing each other and smiled all the way to the patio gate. The newspaper was lying there, so I tossed it onto the patio. When I turned, she wasn't smiling any more. Her eyes were fixed on the cars parked down the street. She wet her lips a couple of times.

---You go ahead. I need to stop at the store.

---I'll go with you.

---No!

She was so loud it stopped me cold. She looked down and away.

---I need to go...

I nodded and waited for a kiss I didn't get. Finally, I walked away. When I looked over my shoulder, she was walking to the store with her head down.

She stopped to tie her shoe. Someone in a big black monster of a car must have called to her, because she approached the window

I kept going. In a few minutes, the car passed me. I didn't see her walking down the block. I looked, but I didn't see her in the window either. Most of it was blocked by the body of the driver leaning back.

We were both late to rehearsal, but she was later. Her eyes got a funny look when she saw me waiting at the stage door. I plucked a flower from the bed and held it out to her. She turned her head, but I saw the tears.

---Don't do that. Oh, don't.

Before I could say anything, she lowered her head and ran into the dressing room. I heard the sound of crying and huge, gasping breaths. I knocked to see if she was all right but all I got as a reply was a kind of strangled moan.

---Oh, God...

Then I heard the sound of retching, and a few gulping sobs, followed by the sound of gargling. I had no idea what any of that was about.

CHAPTER FIFTEEN

Her lips on mine were an invitation to a union more complete than any I had ever experienced in my life. A small pulse beat in her throat and her heavy- lidded eyes were a smoky old gold in color. Her lips flew across mine in short piercing touches that caressed and stung at one and the same time. It was like being delightfully nibbled to death by a small, soft animal.

It was a damn shame we were on stage and she was acting.

On the bright side, she was electric. She communicated every nuance of the script. When I was on stage with her, I thought she was speaking to me alone. On the less bright side, all the other actors were watching in the audience so there was no way to rip off her clothes and have my wicked way with her on the spot.

On the other hand, I have never in my life ripped off anyone's clothes and had my wicked way on the spot. In sixth grade, Sara Middleton ripped off *my* clothes at a party. She didn't have her wicked way with me, because neither of us had a clear idea exactly what that entailed. A few years later when we knew more, well, her wicked way and my wicked way had a lot in common and we shared our knowledge.

When I had an exit, I was able to stand in the wings to watch Bryna play a scene with another actor. It was disheartening. She looked at him as if she was speaking to him alone. I was contemplating suicide when she saw me standing in the wings and winked at me with her upstage eye.

I loved being on stage with Bryna. Hell, I loved being with Bryna. Between the play, and my investigating, and her theatre duties, I hadn't seen nearly enough of her. She gave indications that it wasn't one sided, but there was a reserve that had risen. I had the feeling that we had progressed further, faster than was usual with her and she was scared by the pace of our relationship. I began to realize she really didn't do...what we did...as soon as...we did... It was possible that she was so unsettled by the night we spent together she needed time to process it. I did.

At any rate, she shied from any suggestion we return to her place for drinks or lunch or, ...what was on our minds. Nor would she go out to eat, or for drinks, not even her disgusting carrot juice. I had no idea where we were going and I think she didn't either. It didn't interfere with work. I like to think I'm a professional, and I could see how dedicated she was with anything she set her hand to, but it added a level of tension to rehearsal that was going to have to be addressed.

You could tell Don was amused by all the teen age pining. I think he did his part for *l'amour* through the number of times we rehearsed our scenes. I certainly wasn't about to complain about how many times we worked the love scene.

We spent the breaks together. The rest of the cast gave us a lot of space. We were an "item" and theatre folk love "items." Rehearsal can be boring with all that repetition. Gossip adds a little spice to the proceedings. Nobody knew me well enough to tease me, but Bryna was getting her share of good- natured girl talk, which probably got a little explicit based on the surreptitious giggling and blushing. She would never say what it was about, but I can't say it was a detriment. After those sessions, I would get a little squeeze when no one was looking.

I didn't know what kind of commitment we could have. It was possible that, when passion burnt out, we were headed for a platonic relationship. Though that would be a disappointment, I liked her company so much I would settle if I had to. It might even be best. I wasn't planning to stay after my questions were answered, and it would be asking too much to expect her to give up the life she had for my limited prospects. I didn't even have a reason to believe she wanted anything more than one night.

Despite the reputation of actors as horny rabbits, this was a first for me. Backstage romance, yes. Lust in my heart, well, I'm male. This was different. And I was confused by her feelings as much as mine. I had to think she wanted a replay of our night as much as I did, but if we never went to her apartment that was going to be difficult. I couldn't suggest we go to Don's. Besides the awkwardness of him in the next room, there was Marc. What his nose would do while I did what I wanted to do was an image that didn't bear thinking about.

That left lunchtime trysts on the Equity cot. Given my "no sex in the theatre" standards, all we did was snuggle and kiss, though I got in a little fondling that she didn't object to. End of lunch always found us seated across the stage from each other running lines. The first day, Don lifted one eyebrow and turned away to hide a smile when he walked in. The cast never noticed anything. They were sated with food. Actors are pretty self-involved. Away from a spotlight, they don't notice much. Since we never ate, lunch breaks left me hungry in more ways than one.

The day before dress rehearsal, when the ASM called lunch, Don invited us to his apartment for salads. When we got there, he put Marc on his leash and told us not to wait lunch for him because he had errands to run. Bryna looked away but gave a nod and said we would manage. Don flipped off most of the lights when he left. I was being treated like a teen-aged lover. I should have objected, but I was too caught up in being alone with Bryna. I went into the kitchen to fix the salads, because I knew where everything was. Lunch was ready in a little more than a jiffy.

It doesn't take me long to eat a salad. She picked at hers. I took the dishes to the kitchen and she called out she was going to take a nap. I gave the dishes a quick wash and dry. When I went into the living room, she was lying on the couch so I bundled some pillows under my head and stretched out on the floor. It was quiet and I could hear her breathing. It was a nice sound. I dozed, but she had a very effective way of waking me. A line of kisses across the face ending at the lips will do it every time.

I opened my eyes to see an ivory glow hovering in the air above me. I cupped the back of her head, drawing her down to me for a proper kiss and let my hand slide onto her nape. And then her back. And down to her waist. About mid-rib, I realized all I was touching was skin. To be on the safe side, my hand continued until it schussed over a soft round slope. She was starkers in Don's living room.

Her face inches from mine and that slow, maddening smile was gleaming at me.

---Hi.

I was as suave as suave could be.

--- What the hell?

---I thought we might pursue that really bad idea that turned out to be so good.

---We're in Don's apartment

--- He won't be back anytime soon.

She set about getting me to match her state of undress.

---You can't be sure.

---Yes, I can. I told him to take at least an hour.

Well, a quickie in Don's place wasn't what I wanted. I realize I'm a disappointment to men everywhere, but I thought too much of her to play hit and run.

---OK. If you're going to have your wicked way with me...

---Damn straight I am...

She stopped for a thorough kissing before she continued stripping me.

---Can't we go back to your place?

She sat back on her heels, and I thought I saw moisture in her eyes before her head turned to the side.

---Maybe we shouldn't make love at all...

I brought her face back to me.

---Hey, I do, but I want it to be right.

Well, that opened the floodgates, so I took her in my arms and tipped her face up.

---You don't want to go back to your place.

She dropped her head and shook it slowly.

---Can I ask why?

Her lowered head moved even more slowly. I brought her close and she straddled me, legs extended on either side, head on my shoulder, tears rolling down. I passed my hands over her bare back.

---OK. Look...If being with me is a problem...I'll leave you alone. I don't want to, but I will. Do you want that?

Her head rolled on my shoulder in a negative that relieved me. I tipped her face up for a kiss that turned into something more. I got lost as I always did when she kissed me.

The only possible thing to do under the circumstances was to pick her up in my arms so I did. It was a very romantic moment until my feet got tangled in my clothes and I fell, depositing her on the couch. Fortunately, she has a springy butt so she was up and on her way to the bedroom before I was untangled. I raced to the door to find it empty. Then she jumped on my back and I fell on the bed. There was a lot of laughing and tickling and tangling and untangling. And we found that place we most wanted to be, where we fit together, one, not two, and the world assumed its proper place in the universe.

Making love with someone you love makes for a happy lunch break. Of course, making love in Don's bed gave me pause, but we changed his linens afterward. That counts, doesn't it?

I was doing my studious actor impersonation when he came back, keeping my head in the script. He didn't say anything though I suspect Bryna's red face and lowered eyes may have been a giveaway. I gave away nothing, except for the fact that the script I studied was upside down. He polished off a quick sandwich and excused himself to change his shirt while Bryna and I tried not to catch each other's eyes. I heard a roar of laughter from the bedroom and he came out holding a flower between his fingers.

He gave it to Bryna and started down the stairs.

---You're welcome.

I almost said "for what" but then I turned to see her red face.

---I left it on his pillow as a 'thank you.'

However, shy she was about making love with me in her apartment, she wasn't afraid to let Don know we used his bed. It was a puzzlement.

Rehearsals flew by. When everything about a show worked to perfection, there aren't many things as good. After the last rehearsal before opening, we left in high spirits. On the sidewalk in front of the theatre, Bryna spun around in a circle and jumped up, her legs wrapping around my hips and her lips on mine. The cast streamed by with a few "oohs" and "aahs," but it was good natured. Bryna waved to them, legs around me, my hands cupping her butt, her eyes shining.

I carried her down the street like that. From time to time she nibbled my ear or planted kisses on my neck. I could deal with those but then she braced her forearms on my shoulders and it was hard to walk with her pressed to me, bobbing slowly.

---You know what you're doing to me, right?

Wicked eyes gleamed. A sensuous mouth smiled. A golden head nodded meaningfully.

She laughed and I smacked her on the butt. The laughter stopped. She slipped out of my arms. When I turned her face to me, it was set and dead.

---You OK?

--Your slap hurt a little.

I didn't believe that for a minute. I looked over my shoulder, but I didn't see anything, except for the back end of a black car turning the corner. I tried to make a joke about the butt slap, but she started walking so fast I had to run to keep up. I stopped her at the corner, but she wouldn't look at me. It was hard to hear her voice when she spoke.

---I have to get home.

---I'll walk you.

---No!

She took a long breath and raised a white face to me.

---Go back to Don's. Take a nap.

A slumped figure, very unlike the vibrant person I knew walked slowly down the street. I called to her.

---Where are you going to be?

She stopped, a tiny, lonely figure among the rococo wrought iron balconies of the French Quarter.

---I'm going to be in bed.

Her eyes were diamond bright and she had to control her breathing.

---I'm going to be in bed all afternoon.

She hurried away. I resisted the urge to run after her, but still.... There was something wrong. She obviously didn't want to talk about it, but I was worried.

I didn't nap. I thought about people I had to talk to which made me frown, and I thought about Bryna which made me smile, and after so much thinking, I did doze off.

I needed the rest.

Bryna needed the rest.

Well, it was good that she would be in bed all afternoon.

CHAPTER SIXTEEN

Opening nights are the pits; I don't care how good you are or how well you've rehearsed. It's jumping into the shark tank with raw meat taped to your privates. I wanted to have a pre-show meal with Bryna and be nervous together, but she said she needed to be alone. Well, I understood the feeling, even if it left me bereft. I had to respect her space. If you don't respect an actor's space before an opening, the dressing room dramatics may beggar what happens on stage. The thing is, I liked being with her. Her cool beauty soothed my eyes and calmed me, while her presence got my heart beating and my blood flowing.

I saw her before the curtain went up, face gleaming in the backstage dark. She seemed frail and alone. I took the risk of going over to lift her face and plant a light kiss on her lips. She met me, opening for a deep and extended kiss. She pressed against me in silence a long moment, then drew back, smiled an over-bright smile and lifted a thumb.

The first performance flew by, and I remember every moment of our scenes together. She was magic. It was magic being around her. It was magic looking at her. Magic was everywhere she was.

At curtain call, her face was flushed and she held my hand tightly. We bowed several times and the curtain finally closed. The cast patted us and said kind things and finally we were alone. I was preparing something suitable to say when she threw herself in my arms for a kiss that led me to hope vanished clothing and wicked ways would soon follow, but I'm not that lucky.

---You know, you're a whole lot better than I was told.

I hoped that was a double entendre and I hoped it was true. I tipped her face up.

---Why the hell do you paint scenery and stage manage? You belong in One.

I grabbed her in a bear hug. Maybe I grabbed too hard because she gave a little cry. I asked if I hurt her and she shook her head. I let my hands run over her and found a spot that made her wince. I peeled back her blouse to expose an ugly bruise. I was aghast that I had gotten so rough. That damn Equity cot. They should insist on bigger ones.

I told her I was sorry. She gave me a quick kiss and said not to be silly. I promised I would be more careful in the future. Her eyes teared up. It was like she wanted to tell me something, but we were interrupted by Don who took us each under an arm. We stood like that a moment then he planted a kiss on my forehead and swallowed her in a huge embrace. She stepped back, a sheen of tears in her eyes.

---Thank you.

---No. Thank you both.

The house manager came bustling back to call Don to his front of house responsibilities with the people who provide the money to keep the place going. It was one reason I could never be a director. An actor can mumble platitudes and escape to the safety of the dressing room. A director has to pretend to care what the moneybags have to say. He started out front to meet and mingle, which is the part of the job I always hated most, and then he turned back.

---Of course, you have to do it again next weekend; otherwise, it's a fluke.

I faked a kick at him when he left and turned to Bryna. The smile was gone and she had a piece of paper crumpled in her hand.

---We need to change.

The abrupt switch from the adrenaline high of performance, to say nothing of the warmth she had displayed for me, kept me from saying a word. Her eyes were speaking, but all I could read was a mix of pain and hurt, with maybe a dollop of fear.

---Can I undo any buttons for you?

---Jeff...I...no thanks...

With a flicker of her lips, she set off quickly for the dressing room and I followed more slowly, trying to process what just happened. I don't give up easily, so I quick changed and headed down the hall to the ladies dressing room to ask her out for coffee, but she said no. I thought it was post performance *triste,* so I didn't press it. She also refused my offer to walk her home, a little curtly. That was carrying performance energy to an extreme, but I said OK.

I had my own energy to work off and I did it by walking rapidly and repeatedly around the cathedral. The nervous energy from a performance lasts a while. When you go in on short notice, it increases exponentially. When you've performed with someone you found as exciting to be around as Bryna, on both a personal and professional level, the energy could move the entire French Quarter out to Pontchartrain Beach.

Rounding the corner of the cathedral on my fifth or sixth trip, I saw Bryna emerge from the theatre. I raised a hand to hail her, but her posture was so peculiar the sound died in my throat. Ducking back around the corner, I eased my head out until only my forehead and eyes extruded from the brick. I can be a very sneaky observer.

Bryna looked carefully up and down the street a few times, seemed to take a deep breath, squared her shoulders, and hurried to a long black car the size of the U.S.S. Enterprise—either the carrier or the starship. It wasn't Scotty who beamed her up.

The interior light was on and off so quickly, and I was so far away, I couldn't even make out a body type, much less a face. I wondered who it could be. Whoever it was had more money than I did. The damn car was roughly the size of my apartment.

They sat there so long I almost decided to continue my walk and, maybe, casually, pass by. While I was debating the merits, the horn went off and I saw Bryna's frightened face in the window. A hand rose to grip her head, bringing her slowly down until I lost sight of her.

After a moment, the headlights came on and the motor turned over. The car went into motion in a virtual idle as it moved down the street. After about half a block, it picked up speed, drove past me, and pulled off into the night. I saw a vague outline of a man's head next to a curious, bowed shape.

I decided to cry myself to sleep.

CHAPTER SEVENTEEN

A few days passed with no activity. The theatre was in recess until the next performance. I hadn't tried to see Bryna because opening night, the part after the show, was too vivid a memory. Don finally told me I needed to go out because my moping was depressing Marc. Marc let off gas to reinforce Don's comment, so I left. There was a visit I hadn't made yet, and it was a good night for it.

I looked at the chalked sign on the wall by the door of a small bistro in the Marigny near Washington Park that proclaimed, "Carlo Plays." I hadn't heard "Carlo" play for a long time, so I decide to catch him. It was time for the early set and I pushed through the glass front door that had probably once opened onto an Italian market or a Creole apothecary shop. You never know in New Orleans. There's so much living that's gone on in these streets that everything's recycled, and what was old is forever new.

Ahead of me was a bar, but I turned left. Along one wall there was another bar with a hole cut through the wall to the main one in the other room. A few stools lined the bar and a few tables sat by the plate glass windows for those who wanted to see outside or be seen grooving on the music within. The other wall and the area in front of the stage sported old theatre seats that looked a little precarious, but had served for a long time. I imagined they would last for the rest of the night. Directly ahead was a small stage lined with electric red curtains, and sitting in the center with a guitar on his lap and a stool with a glass of wine on his right was Carlo, eyes half shut, singing his folk /jazz /blues /rock into the night.

His music was eclectic which makes it more New Orleans than all the canned jazz they peddle to the tourists, because New Orleans has always taken what it found: food, music, architecture, or people and put its own stamp on them so they could never be found anywhere else, nor could they leave, because to do so is to cut yourself off from the waters that gave you life.

Carlo had tried, but he had come back. We all do. At least, we all will. I was still in flight, but I knew in my liver and intestines that I would be back one day. I just wasn't ready. I still had to try for geographic distance so that I could eventually focus on the fact that I belonged here. Carlo had already figured that out. Either that or he simply got tired of the rock and roll life where the music starts to sound the same and the groupies look the same and the beer on the bus rolling to the next town is never Dixie and it goes down like colored water and doesn't even give the proper buzz.

No matter how much they scream and crowd you for autographs and press their phone numbers in your hands or flash their breasts to be signed or fondled, it can never cover up the fact that you're not making the music you want to make, because that particular music wells up from the gutters and floats in from the River and rains down from the hurricanes, and it belongs to New Orleans and so do you. You have to come back to sing your song. He had.

His face was pale in the few spotlights that lit the stage, but it was the healthy pallor of a man at peace. His tunes had a lilt and the gutsy turmoil of the blues in equal measure, and his lyrics had the wry wit of a man who sees, and the wounded poetry of a man who feels. That he could express it all led me to believe that I was lucky to catch him in a small bar off a major street with no cover and no minimum because he would soon be playing larger venues where it would cost a lot more to hear him. I think it was Frost who said it's tough not to be a king when it's in you. If that was true, Carlo was musical royalty.

I sat off to the side in the back to be as inconspicuous as possible. I wanted to take the time to enjoy him. If he saw me, he'd probably break his set, and I knew I couldn't stay the night. I failed.

About the third song in, he interrupted the tune to do a little riff and sing about June-moon and spoon-croon and I knew I was busted. I had critiqued one of his early lyrics, which really wasn't that bad, but he changed his writing style afterward and always said I had gotten him out of his June-moon period. He would have done it on his own. He was good. I shook my head and he nodded back that he would play a while longer before we visited.

I looked around the room. There was a mixed bag of auditors, but the general age was on the young side. A small creole-looking guy slid into the seat next to me. The woman with him sat even closer. In other circumstances, I might have thought I was being cruised. Or maybe that was flattering myself. I was probably past the pickup phase, though I'm sure I was still devastatingly attractive in a rather used way. Anyway, I knew the guy for a fine jazz singer and Carlo's sometime songwriting partner. His lady leaned to me.

   ---Long time, sugar.

   ---You noticed.

   ---Would have, ten years ago.

See what I mean. It's good my ego isn't fragile. A lesser man would have been crushed. I was only pissed.

   ---Somebody told!

I laughed and gave up. In a battle of wits, I would always be unarmed. She drifted away to the ladies' room and I turned to Cosmo

   ---Good to be back, I said.

   ---Not the way you wanted.

   ---No.

   ---Anything you want to ask me?

   ---Anything you know?

   ---Honey, musicians know everything in this town, but I do need a little direction.

   ---You know why I'm here.

   ---So, you want to know the truth.

I sighed. ---What is truth?

   ---You and Pontius Pilate.

I stopped to applaud the end of a very nice ballad, and smiled as Carlo went into an up-tempo song about a party we had both been to when we were kids.

   ---If there's nothing to know, I go back to my little play in the Midwest. If there is something to know, I'll know what to do.

His head was bobbing and his eyes were glazed. Anyone else would have thought he was on smack. I knew he didn't need drugs. The music he carried inside him was the only high he would ever need.

---Been to the fire house yet?

---Yes.

---They take you for a ride?

---Yes.

---That's what Cosmo would tell you to do. Ask for a ride. If you don't know after that, you never will.

The song ended with a laugh from the audience and a nice round of applause. Carlo took his guitar strap off and announced a break. A few people went up to the stage. Some dropped money in the tip bucket, a couple wanted to buy his record and a few just wanted to be able to say they spoke to him. I could hit the men's room and still have time to kill before he was finished. I signed to Cosmo where I was going and his head bobbed like he was in another world, but I knew he understood.

I went up the half flight of stairs off the main bar and through the little sitting area to the rest rooms at the end of a short hall. Like all men's rooms in New Orleans bars, it was tiny and you had to maneuver around the stall to get to the urinal, which you had to turn your back on to get to the wash basin, whose mirror was smashed. That last point is why I didn't see the guy who hit me. I went down pretty fast. But I did have time to think that I was tired of being jumped from behind. I wondered if rear view mirrors were an option.

Charley was putting a bar towel filled with ice on the back of my head and Cosmo was snapping his fingers and looking off into space.

---You think he tried to hit on a college stud? Cosmo asked.

---If he did my father'll kick his butt.

---Your daddy's dead.

---Wouldn't stop him.

I made coming to noises and they turned their attention to me.

---Can you sit up? Charley asked.

I know you're wondering about the name change, but Carlo was his professional name. To family, he was Charley. He wasn't performing so I shifted gears. Perhaps that sounds crazy to you. You would not be the first to tell me so. It never changed my habit before; it wouldn't now. My linguistic habits are ingrained. So are a number of other habits. Not all of them are good.

I left the Marigny and headed back to Don's apartment, walking through the cool night air of the Quarter. I hadn't had any contact with Bryna since opening night and I missed her. I'd figured out that she was involved with someone, but she had been a bright spot in my stay, and I didn't want to put that aside just yet.

On the chance that she was a night owl, I decided to pass by for a late-night cup of macrobiotic tea and generic flirting. The alley door was locked, but that never hindered Romeo.

The light was off in Bryna's window, but pebbles thrown at the pane always worked in the movies. I stooped to gather a few. In a suddenly quiet night, I heard something that led me to think pebbles would not be welcome.

There were little sharp cries and explosions of breath that assumed a rhythmic pattern. You don't make those sounds accompanied by squeaking springs, if you're enjoying a mushroom burger.

I got a funny feeling in my stomach. Maybe there are people who can face the knowledge that someone you want to waltz with is doing the merengue with another name on her dance card. Given my druthers, I would prefer to be the one to cause those sudden sharp breaths and quick loud cries. Naturally I wondered who the guy was, and then I remembered that aircraft carrier of a car she disappeared into opening night.

Come to think of it a big ass black car had been hovering around since I met her. I'd thought she wanted to be with me, but, if she wanted to be with me, why him? Then I got it. She wasn't cheating on me with this guy. She'd been cheating on him when she was with me. Well, she could have told me. I would have backed off. Probably not.

I hesitated a moment more, torn between the desire to smash something and the heavy sadness on my gut. I thought we had something. Reality was raining down on me from the window. That was going to be hard to accept.

There was nothing to be gained by standing in her patio letting my mind paint pictures to go with the sounds, so I replaced the pebbles on the ground and started for the gate. Before I reached the street, the sounds changed. I'd thought I knew what the sounds indicated and was jealous as hell. Second thoughts were different.

Guttural demands and high pitched, plaintive negatives followed me out. I think the gutturals won, because the high-pitched sounds changed, yodeling up and down the scale as if someone was torturing a cat's tail and ending in a strangled cry. Whoever was sharing her bed seemed particularly demanding.

I thought of registering a protest on her behalf, but, hey, she was the one who chose to cha-cha. She must have known how the dance card would read.

Climbing the gate quietly was not necessary. I lifted the latch. A keening sound that rose to a siren pitch ushered me out.

The long black car like an aircraft carrier was parked a couple of doors away. So that was how she was able to afford the apartment. Tough way to pay the rent.

CHAPTER EIGHTEEN

There is a lot to be learned standing around a green baize table watching a rubber tipped stick push brightly covered ivory balls into leather pockets. Most of it you couldn't tell your mother, and little of it would help your grades in school, but a lot of it might save your butt one day

My eyes focused on the abstract art of the pool table. I watched as the cue ball struck the number two ball, the two deflected to hit the six, which slipped sideways to strike the four ball, after which the two and four balls, with a few final rolls, dropped into baskets at the middle and far end of the table. The brightly colored balls whizzing across the pool table, caroming into each other, and ricocheting off the green banks were like life.

Out of disorder, stability was achieved. I could relate to pool. Come to think of it, it was a lot like theatre. Action filled the empty baize stage and sense was made of things. Of course, the remaining balls on the table sat waiting for another player to hit another ball. Unlike Life, pool and theatre had endings.

Bennie's Pool Hall was crowded, even if there *were* only two people in the room. Bennie was shooting a game with Skinny. It was for fun. Those two never bet because Skinny had a bad temper when he lost. He wouldn't hit you, but he had been known to sit on you until he got his money back. Skinny weighed close to four hundred pounds. Since Bennie weighed maybe as much as 115 after a big lunch, they were positively not playing for money.

In theory, Bennie owned the pool hall. It's probably urban legend that he bought it with proceeds from Skinny's pool games, but I wouldn't be surprised. At Bennie's, every game ended the same way. The pigeon plucked, the proceeds deposited in a back pocket, a down payment on the next Bennie's Pool Parlor or Pavilion. Bennie likes alliteration or he would if he knew what alliteration was.

He didn't care as much as Skinny did about pool, but that lack of interest did not extend to food, though it did to clothing, and hygiene. I watched as he scratched his chin with chalk covered fingers which left white highlights on his dirty blond whiskers. No, it wasn't "surfer blond". It was blond and it was dirty.

An artist was operating the cue stick as I watched. Now, there is a common stereotype of artists as flamboyant dressers with long hair and dirty fingernails, totally unconcerned with the world. Stereotypes are seldom true. And they weren't in this case. Skinny was a sharp dresser. His wife saw to that.

Skinny was trying a tricky masse and I made my voice as loud as I could.

---My villa in Biarritz against your Panamanian cat houses I can whip your ass.

He turned, looking over his mountain of a shoulder.

---I'll play you eight ball and spot you seven balls.

---Sucker bet.

---Hello, sucker.

Skinny cocked a meaningful eye at me and I shook my head. It wouldn't be worth his while. What he could win off me wouldn't keep him in cue chalk for a week. He made the shot of course. Nothing short of a tsunami could rattle Skinny when he was shooting pool. Unless it was his old lady.

Mrs. Skinny weighed maybe 80 pounds and he was terrified of her. The hardest I bit my lip in my life was the night she had him backed up against the juke box, standing on tip toe, so she could shake her finger in his face. She left with the rent money and mine wasn't the only bleeding lip in the place. He threw the cue stick on the table and walked to the bar.

----The way I remember you shoot pool I should ask if you really want to be here.

--- Paul Bunyan says I do.

---Wouldn't want the Big Blue Ox thinking I was uncooperative.

---Babe is the Big Blue Ox.

---That sumbitch is so big he can be anybody he wants to be.

By the way, when Skinny sat on you, he didn't take your money from you. You had to play again. He seldom lost a second time. One night he did. Even Picasso has a bad day. Anyway, this guy kept winning and winning and Skinny got madder and madder. The guy he was playing was close to a coronary. He tried to miss easy shots, but Skinny would have none of it. He had a code. When you rode with the fat man, you played by his rules.

By the time Skinny finally got his money back, the guy was shaking so badly he could barely hold the cue. All he wanted was to escape, but part of the code was that after Skinny beat you he bought a round for the house, including the loser. The guy needed two hands to get his drink down and, when he escaped, he almost forgot to open the door. It would have made a nasty crash, because the door was glass.

Bennie slid behind the bar to draw two drafts and open a Coke. He remembered when I used to drink in his place and wanted no encore performances. I sat on the edge of the pool table and Skinny took up half the bar stools. Bennie walked over to the other table and rolled the cue at balls he set around the table, making every shot. We could talk. Bennie could be very deaf when he wanted to be.

Skinny knew what I wanted, but there were protocols to be observed. We took care of my mother and siblings, with extra time devoted to what a fine woman my mother was, and then we talked about my career, which wasn't easy, because Skinny hadn't the slightest idea what I did except it was "clean" work.

Sports came next and that took a while because Skinny was a rabid LSU fan. The flattest he ever squashed a guy was the time a Bama fan offered his opinion on the Tigers. Skinny also had a profession other than pool, which might be classified as "bookbinding".

If he booked you, you were bound to pay. The most succinct description of life I ever heard was the night Skinny was explaining the birds and the bees to a guy as he held him up by the neck. "You bet, you lose, you pay." Seldom have I heard the secret to life stated as clearly. If you think about it, that pretty much sums up life.

Bennie got tired of rolling balls, so he went behind the bar to make a muffuletta. That is an art in itself. You take a round wheel of bread the size of a discus and split it in half. You load it up with more meats and cheeses than I can name and then you add the chopped olive (they have to be green), pimento and oil sauce. Opinions differ as to whether or not a dusting of grated Parmesan is called for. *De gustibus non disputandum.* Which translates from the Latin as "Whatever Skinny says." The muffuletta was sliced and there was just enough for the three of us. Bennie and I got pieces the size of pie slices in a diner, and Skinny got the rest.

Nothing takes the place of pool in Skinny's order of things except food. We ate in sepulchral silence. He polished off the muffuletta and two drafts, expressing his pleasure with a mighty burp, took a toothpick from the shot glass on the bar and carefully explored his molars, canines, and incisors. When he was satisfied there was not a crumb of muffuletta to be had, he turned to me.

---Your dad.

---My dad.

---Tell me what you got.

--- I just want to be sure.

---Understandable. Commendable. Laudable. But you got nothing.

He was right. Nobody had given me anything to go on. I knew the autopsy report was bogus. I knew somebody was turning the old neighborhood into a version of Berlin, 1945. I knew my dad was looking into Bubber's death. I knew Bryna was bopping someone in a big black car. That had nothing to do with the investigation, but it sure was on my mind.

---What do you want to find out?

---I want to rest easy so he can rest easy. He'd expect that of me.

---Yeah, he would. So do I, and just about everybody else. Suppose you find nothing?

---I find nothing. But I will have done what I was supposed to.

He nodded and his tongue took over the work of the toothpick. He was rewarded with a tiny piece of olive that he examined on the tip of his finger before sending it to join its fellows in his gut.

---Bennie?

---Yo?

---Place is closed.

Bennie locked the doors and turned out the lights and disappeared into the stock room.

---OK. Tell me everything you got.

I stumbled through a summary of the autopsy report and Bubber and the changes in the neighborhood. He waved me to a stop with a snort. He passed a beefy hand in front of his face as if wiping away a cream pie.

---Tell me what you know.

That wasn't much better. There had been some attacks on me on the streets of New Orleans, but that is so yesterday it hardly seemed worth bringing up. It was pretty clear Skinny thought I was wasting his time, and I positively did not want him to sit on me.

---Let's try this. What are you wondering about that brought you to interfere with a man trying to earn a dishonest living?

That was the question, but it was so thin I tried to beat around the bush, until certain monosyllabic grunts had me blurt it out.

---There's people thinking there might be some politician that connects all that up.

---Politician makes sense. Stir the sewer and one floats to the top with his hand open.

---How can I find out?

Skinny reached out a hand and Bennie put a beer in it. I wondered when Bennie came back in. I didn't wonder how he knew to hand Skinny a beer. He was breathing, wasn't he?

--Legit and ill-. Legit. That's you. Talk to your uncle and see where to go in that green ice cube to get some facts.

---Ill-?

---What a stupid question.

He was right. I didn't want to know, and if I knew it would compromise the most valuable coin of the realm. Plausible deniability.

A couple of Tulane students came in and Bennie swooped on them. I would imagine T-Rex looked much the same at lunch time.

Skinny kept an eye on them. I tried one final question.

---How will I get whatever you turn up?

He looked at me with the pity of a man watching a NORD team try to play LSU.

---You won't. I'm not going to see you again, but I may send a Big Blue Ox to talk to you.

---Babe is the blue ox.

I did not know how everyone could get that so consistently wrong. Our schools aren't doing the job. But then, it wasn't book learning I was after.

Bennie tiptoed over, nodding his head in the direction of the door where the college kids stood.

---Uptown guy thinks he's good at 'billiards' you know what that means.

---Yeah. You and Skinny're about to own the fanciest pool hall Audubon Place has ever seen.

---Pavilion.

---Right.

I wasn't feeling productive, so I decided that all work and no play made for a dull, unsatisfying life. I needed to do something satisfying. I'd go to the theatre, which translates into English as *cherchez les blondes*.

I hadn't seen her since the night I stood in her patio holding a handful of pebbles like an idiot while she danced the horizontal two-step with an unknown partner. There was a reason for that. The memory turned my guts to lye. I'd done a lot of talking to myself ranging from a manly, "broads, who needs them" to, "alas, my heart breaketh." Mostly I settled in between the two.

We hadn't been together that long; there was no claim of exclusivity; she was a liberated woman who could dispose of her favors as she saw fit. That last one usually sent me to bed with my teddy bear.

The facts had to be acknowledged and dealt with. I didn't have to like them. Of course, I could have avoided her altogether and muttered about woman's faithlessness. The problem was, I really liked her. I liked her before I loved her, and I had to admit I probably did love her. She was beautiful, talented, with a sharp tongue, and an acute intelligence. It didn't hurt that she had those mysterious gold eyes with a Slavic slant whose depths I could drown in, and a figure that belonged on a pedestal in a museum. There was also a vulnerability that made me want to take care of her, even as I admired her inner strength. I could pass that up out of hurt and spite, or I could bask in her glow as much as I could, for as long as I could.

There were more nooks and fewer watching eyes behind the scenes, so I headed backstage. If I didn't know what a wicked, worthless life I'd led, I'd think the fates were smiling on me. She was in the dressing room in the middle of changing out of her work clothes. If I saw Bryna undressed any more often, I'd have to start paying her alimony. It would be nice to think she waited around starkers in hopes that I'd show up. On the other hand, that would mean everybody was seeing her undressed more often than me, and that made me green with envy.

When I saw her, I knew I would sign on for as much hurt as I had to in order to be around her. I stood in the shadows watching the way the light sculpted her torso. Her eyes rose to meet mine and smiled because she had caught me out, as usual. I leaned in the doorway hoping she might do a bit of posing, but I was disappointed. She didn't cover up exactly, but she seemed selective about what was on view. She tugged a shirt on and floated across the room to me. Or maybe I floated to her. Certainly, there was something extraordinary about the way we came together like iron filings to a magnet.

She settled in my arms like she wanted to be there and I cradled her as if she belonged there. We shared a kiss we were reluctant to beak from.

---I've missed you.

---That makes two of us.

---Why haven't you been around getting underfoot and annoying me?

---Is that what I do?

She smirked and twined around me like a vine enclosing a tree.

---Well, I suppose you're not underfoot that much.

I swatted her fanny and she jumped away with a cry of something like pain.

---What?

---I've got a tender heinie.

---I always thought so.

I got a fanny slap of my own, but I had the feeling that it was mostly to give her time to think.

---I fell off a ladder, so I'm sore.

I wrapped her in my arms as if she was precious goods, because she was.

---Hey, I'm sorry I hit too hard. I'm just so glad to see you I got an adrenaline rush.

---It's OK. It's not you.

I was worried that she had somehow learned about my patio skulking and was feeling embarrassed. I don't know how she could have found out. I certainly told no one. Maybe I'd been crowding her. I got the funniest feeling that a clock was running, and I should make the most of the time I had with her.

---Let's go to your apartment. I'll cook for *you* this time. I'm not a bad cook.

Even as I said it, I knew it was stupid. I doubt either of us wanted to be reminded of her bedroom and what happened there.

---Or we could sit in here and talk.

She was quiet so long I thought that maybe that had been ruled out of bounds, too. Just when I was thinking up exit lines, she raised her eyes to mine. They were speaking, but I had no idea what they were saying. She went on tip toe to plant a quick kiss on my lips.

---Wait right there.

Before I could assent or refuse, she was gone. The thing was, after being away from her, and now with her, it was the emptiest room I'd ever been in. She was soon back though, pulling on her denim jacket as she came.

---Let's go. I only have an hour.

She set off at a fast clip and I hurried to catch up. We babbled as we trotted, catching up on the time since we'd last been together. Awkwardness disappeared. I was just happy to be with her and I got the same vibe back. She pulled up to a sudden stop and I nearly ran into her. I'd been so busy talking that I hadn't noticed we were outside Don's. Pulling my lapels to bring me close, before I could get out a "say what?" she brought her lips to mine in one of those soft kisses I could really get to like. Her eyes dropped and she almost whispered.

---Don said put the striped sheets on when we leave.

Nothing surprises me. That did.

Backing up the stairs she drew me after her with the lightest touch of her fingertips. We levitated all the way to the bedroom where she pulled the blinds to get the room in the blackest darkness I'd ever seen.

---No fair. I love looking at you.

There was something like a catch in her voice, though she was flip enough.

---Maybe there are other things we could do.

Then she grabbed me by the shoulders and pivoted above me.

I don't kiss and tell, but I can't forget a moment that still awes me, light playing on her face, lips parting in that little girl smile, mouth searching mine. Rising above me, face raised to the ceiling.

Posting, trotting, loping, galloping, an ivory blur until talon hands bit into my thighs as she cried out. We froze and then relaxed in a warm union.

We clung together until, with a sleepy laugh, she leaned forward, our bodies folding together, her hands on either side of my chest, her bosom lightly touching mine, her hair hanging down to shield her face. I wish I could have seen her eyes

--- Such a very good bad idea.

I loved spooning together, feeling her breath and rubbing my cheek against her damp shoulder.

---I wish I'd met you sooner.

I lay there, stroking her back and savoring a very special moment in time.

--- I wish we had. Oh, how I wish we could have.

The moment was cut short when I realized she was crying. I sat up and asked what was wrong. All I heard was louder sobs. I reached for the lamp, but she grabbed my wrist in an iron grip.

---No light.

I tried to caress her back, but she arched away. I tickled her, trying to lighten the mood. Nothing worked.

---Whatever's wrong, I want to make it right. I want to make you happy.

---Don't say that. Don't.

She leapt from bed and dashed to the bathroom, her tears loud. I got the lamp on as she was disappearing into the bathroom. Her back was to me. Normally, I would have loved looking at her derrière. Not this time. A purplish-greenish blotch stained one alabaster cheek. That was one really nasty bruise. Bryna had to have taken one hell of a fall.

CHAPTER NINETEEN

Now, I couldn't find my way around civic records with a flashlight, a map, and a bloodhound. Fortunately, I have an uncle who speaks and people listen. So, I was in the recorder of mortgages file stacks with an older woman and a pimply kid. The woman had the wisdom of the ages. The kid was a true believer who was happy to inform me the records were written on parchment in Spanish and French. I panicked until he added--in the eighteenth century. Recent records were computerized, but prior to the advent of the Information Age, it was paper, old, dusty, flaking paper.

It helped that the geographic area I was interested in was limited to a couple of square miles. It didn't help that I didn't know what to ask for. The kid tottered around under towering stacks of paper. The woman chewed gum and filed her nails. Unhappily, the kid was interested in everything and assumed that the world shared his fascination. I didn't, but I wanted to appear polite, read "gain his cooperation," so I listened to miles of twaddle which advanced me not a whit. He scurried off with his dolly-forklift to fetch more tons of paper when the woman spoke for the first time.

---Honey, what are you looking for?

It was a relief to talk to someone whose heart wasn't in the eighteenth century.

---Somebody's buying up a lot of land and razing the property. It looks like the far side of the moon.

---Any idea who?

---Some politician.

She looked at me over her glasses but was too polite to say, "Well. Duh. Who else would it be?" Though she probably thought it.

---That so?

---Seems to be the consensus.

---Why do you care?

---It might have some connection with the death of my father and maybe another man.

Her eyes brightened and she removed the gum from her mouth. She stuck it on the underside of a table and pushed her sleeves up.

---Something different. Different is good. What do you want to know?

---Who's buying? Individual or group? They paying market value? What's going up on the land?

She walked over to a huge map marked in grids.

---Show me the plot.

I sketched the outline with a fingertip and she immediately wiped off the body oils my finger left on her map. Glancing at the map and a file cabinet, she pulled out a stack of folders, reached under the table to retrieve her gum, and plopped it in her mouth.

---That can't be sanitary. I mean you don't know whose gum that is.

---It's mine. I'm the only one who puts it there.

---How do you know it's the one from today?

---What's it matter? It's gum.

I started to say something else but she raised a finger and made a shushing sound. That was the only sound for some time except for my sneezing from all that paper. A couple of times, the kid came back with a box, mumbled something that I supposed were the coordinates for his next box, or the code to a missile silo, then took off again. The woman never acknowledged his presence or absence. She made little clicking sounds with an occasional snort or sardonic laugh.

I tried to catch my reflection in a window. I hoped my nose wasn't red. If I showed up for Don's play with a red nose, I ran the risk of being tried on treason charges or, at the very least, jaywalking. I'd asked who owned the property, but the woman said I should care more about property rights. Since that was Greek to me, she explained. Everybody watches the ventriloquist's dummy, but the man sitting beside him is the one who's talking.

That made sense. I wanted to know whose idea it was, and if it was worth killing for. I started to doze off, kept awake only by a series of my own loud sneezes.

---Sneaky bastards.

My eyes popped open and I sat up straight. She'd found something.

---All I can tell you is the name on the property isn't worth a dime. The dealings are so convoluted that they can't be legitimate. Records are supposed to make things clear. These cloudy up the picture as much as they can. You'd be better off trying to see who pays the property tax and what the real worth of the land is. Not so long ago it wasn't worth much.

---Who's going to tell me that?

---Talk to the assessor. That'll tell you something.

---Can you go with me? You know what to look for.

She looked around at the boxes of files littering the room.

---It'll take the rest of the day to return this and who knows what else he is on the way with. The boy's too keen.

---Why don't you rein him in?

---Works like a mule.

Coming down the hall, the squeaky wheels of a cart bringing still more records were loud.

The cafeteria at City Hall serves good coffee. They'd be lynched if they didn't. I went there with my notes at the end of the day. I had been to the assessor and the planning commission and I knew nothing more than when I started.

Obviously, the land was being bought up by a person or persons who wanted the identity of the owner hidden. The taxes were ridiculously low, and the area was being rezoned to allow for the erection of the Taj Mahal, the Great Pyramid, and Angor Wat. Somebody was expecting to make a lot of money, and they didn't want to share. So, there was a profit motive at work, but I had no idea how it could be tied to my dad or Bubber.

Then I pulled myself up. I was trying to Sherlock when there was nobody Holmes in my head. I didn't have to pull it together. I had to gather what I could and let them what knows how to do the rest, do the rest.

My dad and Bubber didn't fit. What did my dad know? I drank

some coffee. The enamel melted on my teeth. Good coffee. Then a thought hit and I missed the saucer when I put the cup down. It didn't matter. Bubber didn't have to fit. All that was necessary was that my dad thought he might fit. And my dad didn't have to know a thing. All that was needed was that someone think he did.

Sneezing from the molecules of old paper lingering in my nostrils and bronchi, I sat in the plaza outside City Hall's sickly green panels. It's a mistake to color the facade of your building a shade that has not been popular for at least several centuries. A day's attack on my respiratory system had left me with a pile of not much. I was disheartened until I remembered I was a dog's body actor and not Sherlock Holmes.

The only proof of wrongdoing was the bogus autopsy report. You would only fake an autopsy report if you had a pressing reason to fake it. Or thought you had a pressing reason. The question was who had the juice to get it done? In a Mediterranean city like New Orleans, it wasn't a short list. Councilmen, DAs, police, judges. Judges.

Now, there was a word that was turning up frequently. I sat back. Time to let an investigator have a crack at it. I knew someone whose business it was to take scraps of data and weave them into a coherent whole. I was off to play Watson to my new best buddy on the NOPD. But I was not going to bring Ramirez to Casamento's again. The man can EAT!

CHAPTER TWENTY

The sun-struck windows of the precinct reflected the facade of Casamento's. Heavy police brogans scaled the stairs with a light step while younger, lither officers plodded heavily up. In the receiving room, perps and witnesses sat at scarred desks as statements were taken. Donuts in their mouths, detectives typed reports with two fingers. Occasionally, hands reached for cups and swilled down coffee with the weight of crude oil without halting their plodding fingers.

As a taxpayer, I was insulted that I had to kill time because Ramirez was tied up in some meeting. Fortunately, there were idle minds available for a gab fest. Everyone loves to talk about himself, so I engaged them on their war stories, searching for parallels to my case. I learned a bit about police work. There were strengths and weaknesses in the approach. By building a case brick by brick, the evidence for a trial could be accumulated. The thing was, it then went to a DA, and a judge, and a jury.

Now there is the way that is supposed to work, and there is the way it does work. Or not work. Evidence could be misplaced. The DA might plea bargain. The judge could have a loopy view of the law, and a jury was capable of the most sublime wisdom or logic that would be laughed out of a Looney Tunes cartoon. There was a reason Dickens had a character say, "The law are an ass." Shakespeare may have had the best idea," First, kill all the lawyers."

A drawback to police work was that it put no premium on creative thinking. Don't get outside the box. Color between the lines. The magic of life is in the "what ifs" of the world. Frost's "ability to flash off into wild connections." That was my side of the street. I was totally unequipped for what I was doing. But that meant I was not bound by their strictures. What I would do if and when I reached a conclusion, I didn't know. This wasn't scripted. This was improv theatre.

Officially, my father's death was an accident, as was Bubber's.

Coincidence makes such bad theatre. If I was chasing the old wild goose, why was I attracting interest? Who would want Bubber or my dad to have an accident? There was rampant urban renewal for a big, undisclosed, project. They needed the land. Bubber dug in his heels. He died. My father started digging. He died. Accidents do happen. But they make bad theatre. But I already told you that.

I decided to look with the suspicious mind of an actor. If this was happening, why? Money. What kind of person does all that for money? Now the actor steps into One with his kit bag of Character, Discovery, Text and Subtext. What does the guy say? What does the guy do? What do other people say about him?

My father had been keeping odd hours in odd places. My father was a firefighter. Large tracts of underdeveloped land meant wildfires in the offing. Somebody who would burn down half a city was an idiot of Nero-esque proportions. Where could I find sufficient suspects? Almost any damn place I looked hereabouts.

I was looking for someone with money, power, and position. He had to have some muscle to make himself a player. There were several persons who were earning a spot on my most wanted list. This judge, Duplantis, turned up all over the place. Something cold crawled up my leg from the greasy floor and tightened around my rib cage, spreading ice through my veins. Two bastards I'd like to get are really just one bastard? It's pat, but it wasn't theatre. It was life. I didn't have to worry about pleasing an audience. I let the thought circulate in my brain. Duplantis. If he happened to have a big black car, he'd be number one with a bullet.

It was hot in the room and the sun was making me sleepy. I nodded off. "Perchance to dream" and there was little question who would star in my reverie.

The door to a BBC (big, black car) opened and a nattily dressed pig stepped out. It wasn't Porky Pig or a Disney character. It was more nearly a boar, his tusks dripping with saliva. He got out smoking a big cigar he held clenched in his teeth. One hand held a champagne glass and the other arm was wrapped around a young blonde woman wearing a black-and- white-beaded flapper style dress, tight across her hips so hundreds of flashes of lights sparked as she moved.

A line of flunkies flanked the red carpet the boar walked up, strewing hundred-dollar bills that ragged urchins scrambled for. The cigar ash dropped on the neck of one of the children and she screamed. Fists were shaken at the boar by an enraged mob, but a line of police formed a cordon to escort him inside. As he entered a looming black structure surrounded by a moat, a compact stocky figure with a boxer's stance moved to a car. Opening the trunk, he took out a large tool to assemble a structure that rivaled the looming structure. From a tower of the black building, a Coldstream Guard pointed a rifle. He fired and blue smoke came from the barrel, pouring down to shroud the building and the grounds. From the door issued a line of zoot-suited men with Tommy guns and mirrors. They shot into the air, swinging the mirrors so flashes of light blinded the onlookers. The stocky man made for the door but the mirrors kept shifting location and he became lost. I lost sight of him until the crowd screamed, pointing high in the air.

The man lurched from side to side, blinded by the flashing mirrors until his foot slipped and he plummeted to the ground. I ran to catch him but the ground liquefied. I was running in a viscous mass and could only inch forward. A scream erupted from the crowd. When I looked again, the boar stood on a velvet draped balcony, glass in hand, arm around a blonde, smoke curling from the cigar in his mouth, unmoved by what had happened. Rose petals showered down on him and a flight of butterflies circled above him. I shook my fist at him.

---You won't get away with it, you sorry SOB.

Ramirez sounded amused as he slapped my feet off his desk.

---That's what I say all the time.

I passed a hand over my face and brought the office into focus. He handed me a cup of coffee as he settled behind his desk, tipping his chair on its back legs.

---This coffee fresh?

---It was two days ago.

---Close enough.

He had been in a task force meeting, which was why I had time to dream of the big bad wolf and the big bummed blonde. I asked Ramirez for an update and he had to say he hadn't spent as much time on it as he'd hoped. The task force to crack down on jaywalking or something had been claiming his time. Now, I was for that. Jaywalkers will be the downfall of civilization.

Ramirez wanted to know where my thoughts were trending. Well, they tended to linger on Bryna far too much, but I laid out my thesis. My dad was investigating the death of a friend. Somebody didn't like him poking around. They managed to get him dead and fool the world into thinking it was an accident. It sounded a lot like my dream

He looked at me pityingly and I hadn't even mentioned the cigar smoking pig and the big bottomed flapper. Instead, he droned on about motive, opportunity, and evidence, and forensics. I think I zoned out. It wasn't that I didn't respect his work. I just had no aptitude for it. I tried to explain that to him, but he suddenly had a lot of papers to shuffle.

---Am I wasting your time?

If you think movie actors can speak volumes with their eyes you should meet Ramirez. I poured the rest of my coffee into the waste basket where it ate its way through the container, the floor, and may well be heading for the center of the earth. Look out, China!

CHAPTER TWENTY-ONE

The heat off the cobbled streets of the old part of the French Quarter burned right through my shoes. Since the theatre was in production, there were no rehearsals going on. I decided to take the chance that Bryna might be at home.

As I was turning the corner, I saw the aircraft carrier Enterprise pulling away from her building. Apparently, she was on call whenever the mood struck him. It did unpleasant things to my stomach, but there you go. She wouldn't be the first person I knew to make her living horizontally. I just hated that it was her.

The Enterprise disappeared down the street and another BBC pulled out from the sidewalk. Criminy! They were reproducing.

The gate to the alley was open, so I didn't have to use my mountaineering skills. I walked down the long alley to the small patio, working out what I would use as an excuse for wandering in uninvited. I had to use my excuse long before I planned because she was sitting in the patio on the edge of the fishpond, trailing a hand in the water.

I don't think she saw me. I didn't think she saw the fish. I didn't even think she saw the sunshine.

She was almost wearing a kimono. I say "almost" because it was caught loosely at her elbows and trailed over her forearms. One sleeve was acting as bait for the fish, although they weren't biting. I had seen Bryna nude before, but I had never seen her like this

The bruises I'd seen on her made sense. Her reluctance to talk about why I couldn't come by her apartment made sense. That somebody would do this to her made no sense.

I tried to approach as quietly as I could and, when I spoke, I kept my voice as gentle as possible. I didn't want to startle her.

---Hi, I said.

It took a long time for her eyes to focus. I'm not sure they ever did.

---Hi.

She bit her lips as she fished for a name to put with my face.

---Chaussier.

---Right.

She thought some more. Her brow smoothed out and her face softened.

---Jeff.

---Yes. Jeff.

---I like the sound of your name.

Her lip quivered and her eyes welled over, runnels wetting her cheeks

---I slept with you.

---You did.

---I liked sleeping with you. It was like you loved me.

---Maybe I do.

---You shouldn't. I do bad things.

Well, that was getting us nowhere, so I thought I'd try to get her into today.

---Thought I'd stop by.

She got that withdrawn look again.

---Oh. Fine.

I reached for her but she shied away, so I withdrew. What the hell had been done to her?

---You all right?

Her chin ducked into her shoulder and she looked from under her lids like a melodrama heroine.

---I'm not dressed.

She trailed off and I thought it was best to try to root her in reality.

---Feeding the fish?

She studied the pool and I think it was the first time she understood where she was. Her voice came from a long way away.

---I envy them. They don't have to have anything to do with people. People are...not nice...

I couldn't leave her sitting there. I didn't want anyone to see what had been done to her.

---So, what do you plan to do next?

Her eyes tried hard to focus and failed. She bit her lip in concentration.

---I'm not sure. What should I do?

I needed to get her inside before someone called the fool farm to pick her up.

---How about a bath?

She looked down at her body and shivered in the afternoon heat. She spoke from the place she was, wherever that might be.

---Yes. I'm dirty. I'd like to be clean. If I can ever be.... I'm so...not clean...

Her face contorted and tears ran down her face, but no sound came out. I kept the edge out of my voice.

---Clean is good. I'll help you.

I held out my hand. After studying it vaguely, she reached to take it. I had to tug to get her to her feet, but she finally came up. The kimono didn't. It caught under her foot and fell to the floor around her feet. Her beautiful body was covered with marks. I quickly picked the kimono up and wrapped it around her shoulders. She shook a little as I led her into the house.

Cushioning her head on her arms, she sat on a stool at the foot of the tub while I ran a bath. I threw every bath salt I could find in the water which I got as hot as my hand could stand. When it was ready, I brought her to her feet and stripped the kimono away. The steam rose to envelop her. She was Botticelli's Venus, except that she was not rising from the ocean; she was rising from a kind of hell. I placed her gently in the water, cushioning her head against the edge of the tub. Her eyes stayed closed. I took her seat on the stool. I didn't want her to doze. People have been known to drop their head into the water and drown.

In time, her eyes opened with something like awareness, and she saw me through the mist filling the bathroom. Her head lolled sleepily and her words slurred when she spoke.

---What are you doing in my bathroom?

---I'm going to give you a bath.

She gave a sleepy laugh and waved a finger in a circle at me.

---You just want to see me naked. I told you. No peeking.

I reached for the kimono and tied the arms across my eyes.

---Then I won't look.

She gave that sleepy laugh and lolled her head again.

---You can look. I like when you look at me.

I reached for the sponge and soap and washed her clean, being very gentle around the damaged parts.

I found a big towel to wrap around her. It's not especially easy when you're encumbered with a nearly comatose person's dead weight. Leaning her partly on the wall, and partly on me, I got most of her dry, found a fluffy robe, picked her up and carried her to her bed.

When I put her down, the afternoon light was falling across her face so I shuttered the blinds before I turned to go. Her voice wafted from the bed like the whisper of a breeze through trees.

--- Stay with me. Please...?

Her voice was fragile. I walked back to the bed.

---Hold me, she said. Please hold me...

I wrapped her in my arms. She pressed to me and I felt her warmth through each layer of my clothing. I brushed her hair off her face and she gave a little smile. As her eyes closed, her voice was as childlike as her face.

---I like when you hold me...

She drifted into a disturbed sleep. Her brow wrinkling, biting her lip, tossing from side to side, she was somewhere else. I didn't know where, but I knew she shouldn't be there. Her voice was shrill and breathy.

---No. Don't. Don't.

Her voice became an ascending siren.

---I'll let you. I'll do it. I will...Just don't...

I shushed her, crooning in her ear. She calmed and I spoke her name. Her eyes opened like a person emerging from a nightmare.

---Was I dreaming?

It had been more like a nightmare, but I just nodded. Suddenly shy, she dropped her head.

---Sometimes, I dream about us making love.

Well, that would do, so I nodded. Her face got very red. Then her head lifted and she met my eyes.

--- I like when we do. You're the only person I ever...

I pressed my lips to her forehead to staunch the flow of words.

---Don't go. Stay with me.

I didn't have a chance to answer before her eyes grew wild and her fingers dug into my arm.

—-If you want to do me, you can. I won't fight. I'll let you. I'll do it good...

I pressed my lips to her hair and stroked her back gently.

---We can make love another time.

Her tense frame relaxed and a smile bloomed.

---'Make love,' I like that.

I moved her away and held her eyes to root her in the moment.

---That's what you and I do.

Her eyes got bright and her face glowed with happiness.

---Yes, it is. We make love. Lovely love.

She threw her arms around my neck like a five-year-old welcoming Daddy home from work. I eased her back to the pillow.

---You should try to sleep.

Her words were whispered urgently on one long breath.

---Will you hold me?

I stroked her face and kissed her eyelids.

---That I will, I said.

She closed her eyes and I watched a small damaged child until the light faded and my heart stopped pounding. I blew her hair gently at the back of her neck. She smiled in her sleep and snuggled against me. I thought I might doze for a little myself. There was no rush about anything. I only had one thing I really wanted to do. And I positively was going to do it.

I hadn't been good at emotion for a long time which is a funny thing in an actor. The truth was, I let everything out on the stage. There was stuff inside I preferred not to think about. It made relationships difficult. It was hard to count the number of times I was told I wasn't a giving person or that I locked myself away. I never denied it. I even had a pretty good idea why it was true, but that didn't help.

The first person I opened to in a very long time was Bryna. She was someone I wanted in my life because she could complete me. Now someone had shattered her. By shattering her, he damaged me. That was something that needed to be addressed.

At one point, she cried out in her sleep, begging someone not to do something. I spent a lot of time soothing her and whispering in her ear that it was all OK. Her eyes opened and she searched the dark, trying to make out my face. She reached a hand to feel its contours.

---Jeffrey? she asked tentatively.

---Hush. It's me.

---I like to say your name. Jeffrey. Chaussier. You have such a funny name: Jeffrey Chaussier. But I like it.

I thought she had gone back to sleep because she didn't say anything more and I started to get up.

---You're so lovable.

—I'm not lovable.

—-You are so.

—I'm not either

----I think you are. And I think I could...If I didn't... didn't have to... I could because I do...

She didn't finish. I wish she had.

---But I like you to say you love me. Even if I can't. Even if you don't mean it.

Her voice was coming from such a far place that I couldn't answer for a moment. She may have mistaken my silence, because her voice got plaintive.

---Please tell me you do, Jeffrey.

---I love you.

A wonderful little girl at Christmas smile played on her lips and stayed.

---Again.

---I love you.

---Again.

---I love you.

---Again.

In time, I guess she believed me because she went back to sleep. By the time she fell asleep, I believed it, too. I eased my arms from under her. Leaving her wasn't something I wanted to do, but I had urgent business.

I tiptoed down the stairs to the phone. The first call was to Doctor Jimmy and the second call was to the theatre. Don answered on the first ring. I told him where I was and asked him to come. He didn't ask why. I got the feeling it was a call he had been expecting, though not necessarily from me. I went down the alley to unlock the gate and then I made a strong cup of herbal tea. There wasn't anything harder in the house.

Jimmy got there first. I knew he would. He had a place in the Quarter and knew enough to hurry when I asked him to hurry. I sketched the picture for him, but he was a few strokes ahead of me. He had that kind of practice. I was worried about waking her because I figured she needed sleep almost as much as she needed doctoring. He said it would be possible to look Bryna over without waking her and went upstairs with his little black bag. He came down sooner than I thought and sat looking at me for a second.

---You didn't do that to her.

It wasn't a question because he knew the answer. We went back a long way. I think he just needed to hear himself say it to confirm it. He nodded, finally.

---The salve I put on will help her heal. I'll leave it with you.

Jimmy expelled a breath. He had seen too much. He looked off into space, seeing his emergency room and the wrecked bodies that were tossed like jetsam on his gurneys. It was his impossible task to heal them.

—-I have an idea what he was ...doing to her, but you don't need to know.

He began speaking, not to me so much as using me to get it straight in his mind.

---I don't think she's suffered this over a long period of time. Maybe it started as the guy's idea of foreplay. Something happened to trigger the desire to punish and that became paramount.

He dug something out of his bag and pushed it across the table to me while he wrote out a 'scrip.

---Give her that if she wakes up and get the prescription filled. She might need it.

---You've seen something like this before.

---I work the Emergency Room. Some people can't have pleasure unless they give pain. As time passes, they have to give more pain. Then more. They never back off. It only gets worse.

---She going to be OK?

---The guy knows enough to do his thing without permanent damage. At least none you can see. I wouldn't want to be inside her head when it comes back to her.

His eyes focused and he was speaking to me again.

—-If you can keep her away from whoever did this, you'd be a friend.

---Book it.

He smiled at me as an old friend does.

---From her looks, I'd guess you want to be more than a friend.

---That a medical opinion?

---An aesthetic one.

He took a sip of my cold tea and made a face.

---Take care of her. Call me if she has any specific pain that the medicine can't handle when she wakes up. And, as soon as she can bear to be touched, put this salve on her wounds. It's great stuff. She'll heal fast and she won't scar.

---On the outside.

We tossed off our tea. There wasn't much more to be said, so we said nothing. He left with a wave and I went up to look in on Bryna. She seemed to be sleeping so I didn't bother with the medicine. I stood watching her. The image of her as I had seen her in the blue light warred with the image of her scored body under the kimono by the pool.

My hands clenched into fists, marking my palms with my fingernails. I made a promise to myself and to her in the dark of her room. Then I went downstairs to make another cup of herbal tea.

I heard Don coming up the alley before I saw him. He looked at me with a raised eyebrow. I nodded in the direction of the stairs and he went up. He was there for what seemed like a long time. When he came down, he went to the bookcase in the living area, pulled out *The Canterbury Tales*, removed a fifth of scotch, and stood drinking out of the bottle.

---Who the crap did that?

---Don't know.

---You'll find out.

It wasn't a question. He came to the table and sprawled, his long legs under it, sticking out the other side. I took the bottle and added it to my herbal tea.

---Glad you knew about this. Adds flavor.

---Cast parties. 'Semper Paratus.'

He drank a bit without looking at me and without saying anything.

---It's not good that you were falling in love.

He was right. It wasn't good. But I wouldn't change it.

---What do you know about this? I asked.

He sighed and stretched one of his long legs, pointing the toes, and circling his ankle.

---About three months ago, she said she was moving into a new apartment. I was glad to hear it. The only thing going for her old apartment was that the rats were so big you could put a collar on them and call them pets.

He closed his eyes and pursed his lips in the way he had when he was trying to be precise in his choice of words.

---When I saw this place, I knew she couldn't afford it on what we pay her. I worried how she was paying for it, but it wasn't my business.

I added more scotch to the tea. Herbal tea isn't bad if you flavor it with the proper Scottish herbs.

---For a while it seemed OK. Her work at the theatre was as good as ever, but I still worried. Something was wrong. Then she started 'falling,' coming in with bruises. I'm not a moron. I tried to find out, but she wouldn't open up to me.

He took the bottle back and moved about half of what was left down his esophagus.

There was stuff I had to bring out into the light of day and Don was the one person I could talk to. He would understand without blaming. He didn't need to. I was doing a good job of that myself.

---She must have thought it was safe to be with me. Maybe he was out of town or something. So, she let me into her life. He found out about us and decided to teach her the cost of wanting a life of your own.

I snatched the bottle from his hand and took a big slug. I coughed up about half of it. I just can't drink any more, but I was bitter.

---I had the fun. She paid the bill.

His snorts were more eloquent than some people's soliloquies.

---You're not the one who turned my apartment into a motel. She told me how much she wanted to be with you. She looked like Christmas when I offered my place. She couldn't stop saying how much it meant to her.

He took a long drink and his face set.

--- The second time, she was almost desperate. I couldn't have refused, even if I didn't have feelings for both of you.

He nodded his head, not looking my way.

—-I think she knew what would happen.

Neither of us could look at the other.

—-She knew what the guy would do to her.

Don closed his eyes. In my case a cobweb high in the corner was a subject of study.

---She wouldn't let me see, but I caught a glimpse of a bruise. She said she fell.

Don's eyes could be like stone when he wanted. His voice got equally stony.

---I didn't know this was happening. I can't imagine anyone taking someone like her and using her like this.

---I've seen his car. He's got money. You got money you got power. You take what you want.

The next was hard to say, so I sipped at my tea.

---For some reason, she gave it to him.

The implications of that were not pleasant. Why did she let him? Why would anyone? The guy liked to take by force. And she let him.

Possible reasons went through my mind and they were unpleasant enough to make me drink some more tea. I tried to work it out along the lines of the scenario Jimmy had suggested.

---He got off by inflicting pain. When he got mad because of...me...He decided to see how much she could take. He never saw the steel in her. He pushed the envelope. She didn't resist. He pushed further. She endured it. He couldn't break her. He used her to satisfy every fantasy he could think of. She's in real danger, you know.

---That your opinion?

---Mine, and Jimmy's.

---Jimmy should know whereof he speaks. That Emergency Room is a damn butcher shop.

—-Dr. Jimmy said those guys were good at hiding ...what they do...

No wonder she hadn't wanted to let me in her life. There was no way she could trust anyone. I had to wrap this up and get away before I lost it.

---From what I can see, the only thing left is snuff stuff.

---You think he'd do that?

---You saw her?

---I think he'd do that.

The bottle was empty. He'd need another one to hide, but I wasn't sure if there'd be cast parties here in the future.

---What can I do?

--- Stay with her. Here's a 'scrip' to get filled. Have them deliver it. I'd rather she wasn't alone.

He nodded. I went up the stairs to see her one more time. The covering robe had slipped off and she was nude from the waist up. In the darkness the marks didn't show, just the white gleam of her. I found a light blanket to spread over her and brushed my lips through her hair. When I went down the stairs Don was making a cup of herbal tea.

---That stuff'll kill you, I said.

---The liquor store on the corner delivers. I'll make it.

I started for the door and stopped. I spoke with my back to him. I didn't want him to see my face.

---Don't let her know I was here.

---You think she won't remember you?

---I hope she won't remember the entire evening.

---I'm sure she'd like to know you took care of her.

---Tell her it was you.

He would take good care of her. When she woke, he'd have a lie ready as to why he was there and she would trust him utterly. As I did.

He had a gruff exterior, but a loving heart. I had a loving exterior. You didn't want to see my heart just then.

I let myself out the gate. Down the street a BBC was idling at the curb. I saw red and headed straight for it. Not the wisest thing to do, but as I said, I was seeing red.

I'm not sure what I would have done but the two lean-faced men in the car looked at me incuriously, so I just nodded and went on my way.

Wonderful. I was hearing footsteps everywhere and now I was seeing big black cars everywhere.

I finally got to Don's and did something I hadn't done for a very long time. I set out to get drunk.

I stared at the wall that held the picture Bryna painted.

The garish splashes of color reminded me of the marks on her, plague stains on an alabaster Madonna.

Every time I closed my eyes, a nightmare image appeared. I tossed but I couldn't rid mind mind of the imagesd.

Bryna with a hose washing paint away.

The water became acid melting her flesh. Her vision, tinted by blue light, was marred by red slashes across her breasts and belly.

In a perverse repeat of the time I saw her changing in a dressing room, the mirror showed flesh flayed from her back and bottom.

She was screaming and the sound echoed in the room, merging

with Marc's bugling to create a cacophony that shattered the glass in the skylight above the couch.

It fell in shards and I was stabbed by a rain of icicles that pinned me to the couch like a butterfly.

I woke in a sweat, uncertain where I was.

When even liquor doesn't work, there is no choice but to deal with life.

CHAPTER TWENTY-TWO

It was morning by the time I let myself out the cypress board panels that made up the door to Don's apartment building. The air had that watery feel wind blowing over the river lends the breeze. Draping over my face like a barber's towel, it carried the morning smells of the Quarter. There was the sharp musky smell of roasting coffee and the scent of patio-blooming flowers so sweet it cut the chicory taste of the coffee. It was a heady mix that didn't quite cover the odor of rancid garbage wafting from the gutter's catch basin or the acrid tang clinging to the brick wall where somebody had thrown back to Bourbon Street the largess he had imbibed the night before.

I tripped over the legs of a kid stretched on the sidewalk by the door. I suppose, after a night in the Quarter, any place was a good place to lay your head until it was able to return to your shoulders without throbbing. He had on dirty jeans and a grey sweatshirt. That was strange, given the heat, but I wasn't his tailor. I looked up and down the block. Don's street was not heavily traveled, so it was unlikely the police would be by. Still, we've all been there, and I didn't want him to end up in the drunk tank because his gullet didn't know the meaning of the word "stop." I'd had trouble learning that word in my time.

There was a recessed doorway a few houses down that would offer him shelter until he came to, so I grabbed him under his arms and dragged him down the block. He was dead weight and his shoes made a heavy scraping sound. When I got him in the archway, I twisted him around to rest his head against the lintel to make him as comfortable as I could. When I saw his face, I knew two things. I had seen him before, and when I last saw him his eyes didn't have that wide glassy stare, nor had his gray sweatshirt been soaking up his blood. It was the kid who had been so nervous about talking to me. He may have been the victim of a random mugging, but he had been left on my doorstep like an unwanted orphan. I couldn't say the two were connected, but I was getting damn tired of the coincidences piling up around me.

Tommy would be at the Cupcake. He might be able to tell me if the kid was into anything bad or if it was his link to me, that brought about his demise. Bad karma was piling up around me and I felt like Ishmael, "Only I have escaped to tell the tale."

The kid was so young. He wanted to be an actor. He had dreams that were now as dead as he was. I wondered if he had a family. There should be somebody to mourn you or you're just a hole in the ocean. The waters don't remember you passed through them. There is no marker saying you were there.

My dad wasn't going to be a hole in the water and I wasn't either. My profession was the most ephemeral of the arts. When the curtain closes, all that's left of your performance is what lingers in the mind of the audience.

Sex was an escape, but it was as ephemeral as acting. I suppose that's why love exists. You cleave to someone in the dark and merge your loneliness with hers. Enough of that. I had things to do.

I walked to the pay phone on the corner and spent some change on three calls. In the first, I was an anonymous good citizen reporting a body on the street. The second was to Jimmy to ask him to talk to his friends at the coroner's office to get the results of the autopsy on the kid. The third went to Detective John Ramirez. It wasn't his district but I had a feeling it was part of our problem and I wanted to have another heart to heart with him.

When I was leaving the phone booth, I saw a familiar black car in the area. It was beginning to bug me on many levels. I tried to keep an eye out but I'm not very good at spotting surveillance. That might have to change. It looked like the BBC with two men in it. They followed me as I walked to the Cupcake.

Tommy was upset. The kid was no great shakes as an actor but he was kept around like the theatre cat. He lightened the day and performed a few chores. Tommy's wife and son took it hard too. The son let off a string of curses and smashed up a couple of chairs. Tommy never said a word to him about it. The wife was worse because she had her maternal feelings invested in the kid.

Mrs. Tommy was good at picking up strays. She nurtured and developed their inherent nature and made them a part of her world. Tommy and her son were prime examples. Left to themselves, I couldn't say where they would be. Together they were a family unit. When I thought that, I felt better about the kid. He wouldn't be a hole in the water. He would be mourned because he was loved. That's no small thing.

The BBC, which had become my mental shorthand for the big, black car, sat outside as I sprawled in a chair in Ramirez' office. Chairs in a cop house are not made for sprawling. We waltzed for half an hour, each trying to find what the other knew. He was good at hiding what he knew. I was good at not showing I didn't have a damn thing. I had the feeling we were on the same page, but he was too cagey to show it and I didn't have his experience at interrogation to get it out of him. In the end, we bowed like gentlemen, secure in the knowledge that the dance would go on. Neither of us was a quitter.

The way Bryna looked when I found her gnawed at me. I couldn't reconcile the damaged creature of that night with the naiad with the hose or the blue sculpture in the wings. I couldn't believe people did that to other people, which was naive of me. Between Hitler's extermination camps and Stalin's gulags, there was plenty of evidence of the capacity of mankind for inhumanity. History is divorced from us. It sits in an "out there" that doesn't impact on our "here." Until the day it does.

Based on my halting and incoherent ramblings, Ramirez couldn't do much. I couldn't bring myself to get into specifics. He had the idea of letting Don and Doctor Jimmy be his sources of information and I seized on it as an out for me, and a more efficient way for him to proceed.

The whaleboat was still idling outside when Ramirez walked me to the door.

This time it was a single guy, so I didn't have to be polite. I knew what he'd been up to. I was sore enough to flip off the car as he pulled away. Ramirez lifted an eyebrow.

I didn't want to explain too much so I just shrugged.

---Damn car's been around too much. It's been hanging around me and a...

The image of Bryna in her almost kimono that almost covered her marks stopped me. The sleeves trailing in the water of a pool she couldn't see, populated by fish she envied, flooded me with bile and I literally had to swallow or I would puke.

Ramirez was too smart to swallow my half-hearted lie, so I tried a version of the truth.

---Been seen around the place of a friend of mine. I've started to wonder who it belongs to.

I knew Ramirez was both smart and cautious so he did both.

---Hell, that gun boat? Duplantis.

That name was coming up too often, but in south Louisiana it wasn't an uncommon name.

---From around Lafayette?

His level, uninflected tone let us both know that he was a fisherman. He would dangle bait, but he wouldn't strike too soon.

---A judge. Right in the city. Office at the courts. He holes up in a big old warehouse. I hear he has a honey pad in the Quarter and a place out by the lake. Local as you can get.

---One of our own makes good, huh?

His dark face grew darker and his voice got deeper. My instinct was looking better all the time

---Nothing I want to say standing in the precinct doorway. Let's just put it, I wish he would set one foot on the other side of the law.

---And if he did?

---Latin people hate good and feud better.

I liked him. I wasn't sure he'd ever see his thirty and gold watch because his sense of justice was too finely honed. If I could bring the strands to Ramirez he would do his damnedest to knit them into a noose for my least favorite jurist. It was a plan.

---Amigo, you go talk to my friends. You just might take a judge down.

Those dark eyes snapped with interest and his mouth thinned to a slit.

---How?

Well, I didn't have the faintest idea, but I did have that one essential of the acting game. I had motivation. I slapped him on the shoulder as I left.

CHAPTER TWENTY-THREE

I didn't know why Tommy wanted to meet in the alley again. The alley had only bad memories. The kid had been so young, and had that same puppy dog look I had when I was young. I didn't know him, but I could see why he would leave a hole in your life when he was gone. I didn't know what had gone down, except I had a sinking feeling that it had something to do with him being seen with me.

Tommy didn't use the "i" today. He was as far from the "i" as you could get. He wore a tee shirt that showed off his muscular arms and torso. There had been times when people mistook the work for the man. Every actor knows the difference except for the ones who've been told they were geniuses. They usually find it's lonely up there with only you and the people who want your money. Because Tommy was a female impersonator, some people thought he was gay, except they didn't use a word that polite. They only saw him in drag, but I had seen his old Marine Corps uniform in his closet. There was no way I wanted Tommy mad at me.

He sat on an orange crate, his hands dangling between his legs. He didn't lift his head when he spoke. I hunkered in the Asian crouch, feet together, elbows on knees, bum a few inches off the ground. You could sit like that all day without getting tired. I waited for him to talk.

---He wanted so badly to be liked, to be needed.

I didn't have anything to say so I didn't say anything. You'd be surprised how often that's a good idea.

---It's my fault. I taught him that doing things for other people gave you value.

I let him talk. Maybe he was right. The kid was looking for a home. He ran errands for the Tommy family and they accepted him. He thought their loving embrace was normal. It isn't. Not in this world.

---I should have taught him better.

I looked away as Tommy took a long shuddering breath and looked at me from the corner of his eye.

---I thought it was silly, you trying to investigate what happened to your father. Right now, I only want to crack heads and get answers.

---I'm not much on cracking heads and I haven't got too many answers so far, but I'm getting into the whole questioning thing.

He sat for a minute. I knew his mind was made up when he asked to see me. Tommy wanted to tell me something he feared was dangerous. He'd held back out of concern for me. The kid's death altered the scales. Tommy wanted his pound of flesh and I was in a mood to give it to him.

---What do you want me to know?

He raised his head for the first time, but his eyes were focused far beyond the alley.

---There's this ass rides around in a big black car.

I was getting really tired of big black cars. Surely somebody in New Orleans drives a snazzy red convertible.

---He drive it?

---Sometimes.

---I've seen it around. Shows up way too often for my taste. You think it's my BBC?

---What the hell is a BBC?

---Shorthand. Ever see more than one at a time?

--- Why are you asking?

---I been trailed by two back mollies lately. One's got a single driver, the other's got two guys in it.

He raised his eyes to the sky. I didn't know if he was seeking divine inspiration or if he was trying not to hit me. His eyes finally lowered and fixed on mine.

---There's this judge.

---Baby, there's a lot of judges, and not all of them are on the right side of the bench at trial.

I'd coaxed a smile from him anyway. His face was less drawn for a moment and that was good.

---This SOB plays with dangerous men and has unsavory

habits.

---Sounds like my man.

---Be careful around him.

---He dangerous?

---By himself, maybe not, but he's been borrowing from people you should only borrow from carefully and he pays a heavy vig.

---Could it be he has lots of fire sales for that reason?

---Something like that. Word is he's wearing out his welcome and their customer relations policy is strict.

I traced a pattern on the cement with the toe of my shoe as I thought.

---These folks interested in me?

---Doubt it, but they are interested in him.

---Both cars keep showing up.

---Be careful. You don't want to be collateral damage.

I thought of Bryna and had to take a minute to clear my throat. The look in his eyes told me he knew more about my life than I wanted. I don't know why I was surprised. Knowledge is the coin of life and the judicious use of it has a lot to do with how happy you are.

---A bent judge with bent tastes messing with men with bent noses. Unsavory, even for New Orleans.

He looked away with a half shrug.

---Thing is, you keep your life in compartments, stuff can be overlooked. Flaunt it and you make business partners nervous.

---You think he's doing that?

---Will an alligator bite your ass?

If Tommy was right it was possible my little problem could be solved without me lifting a finger. That would be OK. I don't especially like to get mixed up with violence. I was always afraid I'd develop a taste for it. Tommy looked incredibly sad. I stretched a hand to rub his shoulder and he raised misty eyes.

---He seemed like a good kid.

---He was.

---What did a guy like that need with a kid like him?

---Cover. The kid was invisible. The guy couldn't afford to be seen. The kid could go anywhere.

---Why is he dead?

Tommy was quiet a long time. I would have tried to speed him up but his eyes were focused on the mansard roofs of New Orleans and tears were rolling down his cheeks.

---I'm going to find out.

I didn't like the tone of his voice. It promised foolhardiness.

---You don't want to do that. You got a wife, a son and a local reputation.

---I can't sit by.

---Yes, you can. Appoint me your Deputy Dawg.

---Why you?

That was a good question. I had no special knowledge and no special skills. But then, if anything happened to me, I wouldn't leave that big a hole in the world.

---Because I'm disposable.

Tommy nodded.

---You might be right.

He didn't have to agree that fast, did he? But he was correct. It had an unsettling truth to it. I had a family (seldom seen.) I wasn't known (except to a few people who were not always thrilled by the knowledge.) And I was never going to pull thirty because I had no career to speak of. (Read my reviews.) There *was* a girl I had hoped to convince I was better than I appeared, but those plans had crashed and burned.

---I need to get back.

---Rehearsal?

---No. We have a wake and a funeral to arrange. He lived alone enough. He's going to have family when he leaves.

I think if I had to have somebody outside the family arrange that for me, Tommy wouldn't be a bad choice. He stood and handed me an envelope.

---What I know, what I suspect, and what I'd like to learn. Take care of it.

---I will.

---I know.

I tapped the envelope against my teeth as he threaded his way through the detritus of a big city. It had all seemed so clear backstage in the Midwest. I'd come home with things to do and people to see. I'd seen most of them. There was one visit I'd been putting off. I hadn't seen Bryna since that night. I didn't want to go there alone and there was only one person I could ask to go with me.

The theatre seemed quiet and empty, even though it was filled with actors and crew and that largest and most important group in the theatre, hangers-on. Still, the space felt empty. It needed the presence of a small blonde with golden eyes and a killer smile to bring life to the place, but she was on "medical leave." I had been avoiding her, which was cowardly, I suppose. A drop by visit was called for. I didn't know how casual I could be, so I was recruiting Don to go with me.

He saw me when I came in, but went on with rehearsal. The show was his priority. Bryna hadn't asked to see me for reasons that bothered me. I knew why I hadn't gone. I was responsible. Whatever had been happening between her and her keeper had been acceptable. Until I showed up with my tongue out and my paws up. The guy must have found out. Knowing, he decided to punish her. That was my fault. I wish he'd come after me. I hadn't forgotten all my training.

Out on the patio, there was a breeze and I let it play over me. Bryna had been willing to make love here, but I thought too much of her. She would have made love in the dressing room, but I thought too much of her. So, because she took me to her apartment, she ended up that month's centerfold in the S&M magazine.

I went back into the lobby. I was having a marvelous time beating up on myself which is a waste of time. There are always people more than happy to beat up on you, if you'll let them. I did the Asian squat against the wall. It was almost the exact place where I asked permission to fall in love with her. She'd been right to tell me not to fall in love with her. In her situation, she couldn't fall in love with me. Or anyone else, for that matter.

That she gave as much as she did proved that women are just flat better than we are when they love you. I took in and let out a long breath as I let my last words play ping pong in my head. I loved her. I was sure of it. Maybe she could love me. I was sure about one thing. The visit was going to be upbeat, even if I wasn't sure what words to say.

Don came out of rehearsal, picked me up with an upward nod of his head, and led the way to Bryna's. I wanted to plot strategy on the way, but all I got were his specialized monosyllabic grunts. No one does monosyllabic grunts better. In consequence, I walked in with no idea of what to say or how to play it. You'd think a director would stage a scene better. All he did was walk in with me in tow. She was sitting in the patio again and the light was doing wonderful things to her hair. I couldn't speak. Don bent to kiss her. She smiled at him, but her eyes were on me and he knew it.

---Hi, doll baby. Jeff here heard you weren't feeling well and wanted to come by to visit. I tried to stop him because I thought it might cause you to relapse, but he ran faster than me so here he is.

Then he left, and I was with Bryna, more covered up than ever. She looked a little pale, but better than the last time I had seen her. Jimmy's a hell of a doctor. Her hair was brushed back, showing her high forehead. It made her eyes look more slanted and golden than ever. She had a half smile on her face, but she didn't move with her usual grace. It was like linkages were missing and she had to plan each move in advance or she would shatter. Since Don had left me high and dry, I was badly in need of a dialogue writer.

---Don says you aren't feeling well.

Those were the last words spoken. She flowed across the patio into my arms and I held her like the fragile, precious being she was. She fit herself to me as carefully as if she was jockeying two space capsules together and one wrong move could lead to disaster. We had embraced passionately, but we had never been so delicately linked.

The movie people have something. On stage, you need a lot of dialogue to convey what is happening. A film gives you a picture that says everything. Fingertips touch faces. The pads of fingers stroke cheeks.

I cradled her in my arms. Once I forgot myself and squeezed a little too much and she smothered a yelp. I apologized for being such a bear and she said I was a big bully, but she pressed her lips to my cheek as she did. I tried to assess the damage to her as surreptitiously as possible. She pressed her forehead to mine and gave a little chuckle. I don't think she knew what I was doing. She thought I was just trying for a feel.

I was almost satisfied she was all right. On the outside. I didn't want to know what she was feeling on the inside. I placed little kisses over her face and neck and she ran her hands over my back and shoulders. Time passed and a kind of peace settled over us. She seemed tired so I carried her upstairs. I got a lifted eyebrow when I stood holding her over her bed. I did my innocent Alfred E. Neumann face which made her laugh, and that was good, but then she winced from her injuries and I felt like hell.

I placed her down as gently as I could and pulled the covers over her. There was so much more I wanted to do, but I was glad I could at least tuck her into bed. She asked me to hold her while she fell asleep, so I stretched out beside her. Her eyes were smoky and her lips had a half smile. As she breathed, her lips puckered out like a baby's because her nose was swollen. She drifted off pretty quickly. I lay beside her for a while then eased up. Her eyes opened and she asked me to come back. I nodded and she fell asleep with that ghost of a smile on her lips. I'd be back. She could book that bet.

Don was waiting on the patio when I went downstairs. He cocked an eyebrow to ask if everything was OK and I nodded. We started back to the theatre.

---She doesn't know I'm the one who found her, does she?

He shook his head. He was in Sphinx mode and I wasn't going to get much out of him.

---Does Jimmy think she's going to be OK?

For the sake of variety, he nodded. It was like working with a radio mime.

---What can I do to help?

He got the enigmatic look of a skinny Buddha, dragged out a cigarette, lit it, and blew a puff of smoke.

---You just did.

When we got back to the theatre, I found a message from Charley that he wanted to see me after I left "my girl's" place. If Charley knew I'd been seeing a girl, the Quarter and the Marigny knew. That bothered me. If "somebody" knew, "somebody' could act on that knowledge. "It's not paranoia if they really are, etc."

I was starting to feel more and more complicit in what happened to Bryna and I didn't like it. It was starting to look like she was far from a peripheral character in my Götterdämmerung. I was pretty set in my own mind that the person of interest was a judge named Duplantis.

He seemed to have had a hand in Bubber, and my father, and the kid, and now Bryna. There was going to be an accounting. I wasn't a dangerous type of character, except for one thing. I had nothing to lose. I also had blood kin and that counts for a lot in New Orleans.

CHAPTER TWENTY-FOUR

When I showed up in Unc's office he took one look, rose and, taking his suit coat from the back of his chair, slipped it on. He didn't even stop. Just went down the terrazzo-floored hall to an elevator that was showing its age. He nodded to a couple of people, bent his head to listen to a constituent, and slapped a passing pol on the back. Not once did he ask what I wanted or why I was there. We walked across the city seal in the lobby and turned left to the parking garage behind the building.

---It's lunch time. Let's go to Ruth's.

By the time we got to his car my shirt was plastered to me with perspiration. He wore a suit and a tie and had not so much as beads on his forehead.

Ruth's has the best steak you ever put in your mouth and when it comes out of the kitchen, sizzling and loaded with butter, it looks like they are bringing you half a cow. I had the junior filet mignon and it looked to be the size of a football. The only thing I had as a side was broiled tomatoes. I needed to give my jaws variety from chewing the filet. Not that there was a lot of chewing involved. It dissolved on the tongue.

I knew my uncle ate here regularly, and it used to be I couldn't imagine why he wasn't the size of a horse. Eating with him today, I learned. He barely got enough of the steak down to trim the edges. Every sorry politician in the room stopped by his table and he had a joke and a greeting, and, sometimes, a few whispered words, for every one of them. I couldn't imagine how we were ever going to talk about *anything,* much less the subject I wanted to talk about. It was a public place with many conversations going on at the same time. I eventually realized that was the genius of the thing. We were out in the open, so obviously we were aboveboard. With that much meeting and greeting, we couldn't possibly be discussing anything of importance. But we were.

I learned that Duplantis had mob backing, earned through light or non-existent sentences or errors that could get a verdict overturned on appeal. I learned that Duplantis was scooping up more real estate than a horde of locusts could devour in a year, and paying for it with the insurance from properties that mysteriously suffered fire, explosions, and other acts of God, if God was an arsonist. I didn't understand.

Duplantis had the money to buy the land, then why the fires? Greed? Maybe, but there are some less-than-legal folks who like a quick return on their investment. Maybe the money was advanced with a quick barbecue the fastest way to pay it back before the vig got too big. If that was so, Duplantis was even worse than I thought. Taking him down was not going to be simple.

As we were getting to the heart of that particular problem, we were graced by a visit from the man himself. The only heads-up I received, was a quick stomp on my toe under the table, and an expansive greeting for Duplantis from my uncle as the judge approached from my blind side. Duplantis sat and my uncle introduced me as an actor. For a few minutes, he engaged in mindless chit chat, and I wondered what he was up to.

---So, you're an actor?

---That's right.

---Hear actresses are tigers in the rack.

I hadn't been sure he knew about me and Bryna, but I couldn't imagine why else a coarse Hugh Hefner showed up at the table.

---Could be. Don't know.

---This little actress I screw, she sure'z hell is.

I knew this game, and I was sure he was good at it. The thing was, I had a face that could show my innermost soul or flatten out like a pie pan under a semi's tire. He wasn't going to get the reaction he wanted.

---Sorry. I'm new in town.

Duplantis had eyes like a boar in the woods, small, mean, and red with malice. He leaned in. He used a lot of cologne, but he needed to double up on the mouthwash after eating a salad with extra onion. He also needed to get further away from me because his spittle was entering my ear canal. He would be the last person whose saliva I wanted in my ear.

---I tell you, boy, ain't nothing like an actress in bed.

I didn't like him. I especially didn't like him drooling on my filet.

---Why? Because she can make even a floppy disk think he's a hard drive?

My uncle applied his foot to my toe under the table again. It hurt, but not as much as my jaw muscles from clenching my teeth.

---I get more stuff than you ever dreamed of.

Even a poor actor knows something about control, although I *did* have to pat my lips with my napkin so he couldn't see my pointed canines that wanted to tear his throat out. He leaned in.

---This piece I'm doing ain't got a big rack, but she got one real fine ass.

I dug my fingers into the hard wood of the chair to release the energy I wanted to expend on his face. Unc's foot was doing a clog dance on mine to remind me to cool it. Short of punching Duplantis, I needed a diversion. I thought a Restoration comedy voice might work. At any rate, it would give me a chance to practice my Restoration comedy delivery.

---So, the lady in question is exquisitely formed.

His eyes got very flat. In their depths, I saw the little boy who tortured small animals. My feint hadn't worked. He *knew*, and he was going to keep the needle in, like pinning a butterfly to a board. He leaned back, playing with my words as if they were a foreign language.

---'Eks-kwa-set-lee formed.' Don't know about that, but she's one great damn lay.

His eyes fixed on me, daring me to let slip a sign of interest in who he was.

--- 'N I get it any time I want. Anywhere. My place in the Quarter. In my car. On the Fly in Audubon Park.

To my credit, I didn't move a muscle. To my shame, it was because Unc had my forearm in a death grip on my knee.

---Down to the coast, but she din't see no sand, except maybe what was in the bed I was holding her face in while I rode her 'eks-kwa-set ass.

Unc cut in, clearing his throat loudly, making a show of wiping his collar and patting his face with his napkin. He gave that rumbling laugh that told the room pleasantries were being shared.

---For God's sake, Judge, I'm too old to listen to this.

Duplantis didn't give up easily. Perspiration beaded his forehead and dampened his shirt under his armpits, but he was going to get his pound of flesh. Good luck with that. I deal with producers and agents all the time.

---You ever shift gears with a head in your lap?

I pulled back as far as my chair would permit because he was too tempting a target. I could smell the martini beneath the onion odor and examine his fillings if I wanted. I didn't.

My uncle either saw me tense or knew me well enough to know what I was about to do. He laid a casual hand on my biceps that had the strength of a steel claw

---Well, I'm sure Jeff here is as envious of you as I would be if I was younger, but as a practitioner of the Faith, I can't listen to much more of this or my Saturday confession will be such as to give my good parish priest a coronary.

It was amazing. My uncle's hand looked to be resting lightly on my arm, but when I got home, I had purple finger marks across my bicep. I kept my eyes on Duplantis. Wet lips smacked and a thick tongue swept over his mouth.

---Wanna see pictures of her nekkid ass in action?

I was fingering my steak knife, calculating the angle to his guts and my chances of getting out of there without a handcuff bracelet. They weren't good.

At around that point, my uncle's voice rang out in a way that turned every head in the place.

---Well, hello there, Archbishop!

I didn't look and Duplantis didn't look, but everyone else did. Unc got to his feet, dabbing his lips with a napkin.

---Your Eminence, could I ask you to come over here a second?

A figure in red appeared in the corner of my eye. Duplantis and I were still locked in a death gaze that he held as long as he could, but no judge was going to stiff the archbishop so he rose to kiss the ring. There was a certain amount of politicking before Duplantis left. I sat gulping down ice water to cool the fire raging through my guts. My uncle was bantering with the archbishop and half the restaurant was laughing until the archbishop pulled away to go to his own table.

My uncle gave a final wave and sat. He returned to his food, seemingly without a care in the world, speaking around chomps on his steak.

---Were you about to do something foolish?

I lifted a piece of steak I never tasted, though I chewed and swallowed.

---Could be.

He nodded his head and took his time carving another piece. His eyes circled the room as he chewed and dabbed his lips with a napkin to cover his words.

----Sorry your girl's with the bastard.

So much for stealth and subtlety. I was so out of my league with him.

---How'd you know about her?

He gave a big laugh and patted my shoulder.

---I know everything worth knowing and a few things that aren't.

I'm good at stating the obvious. I dropped my fork and stared at the plate.

---He knows how I feel about her.

A snort was smothered by another drink of tea

--- Sick bastard. He's used women like this before. Maybe's just rubbing your face in it.

My uncle cut another sliver of steak and swirled it through the juices.

---It's likely he is involved with people you wouldn't want to get involved with.

---They wouldn't happen to drive around in big black cars, would they?

---That's a Phi Beta Kappa key in some circles.

I knew what that meant, just like I knew Unc drove an old green Buick

---Would these choirboys be interested in me and my girl?

---They tend to be interested in money. Especially their money that other people are being too free with.

---Like Duplantis?

---Want some more iced tea?

Suggestions were piling up that made me wonder what alligator pond I was wading in.

---Be careful, Jeff.

He put his knife down and dabbed at his lips with a napkin which had the effect of keeping any lip readers at bay.

---Get her away from him, if you can. If you want to take him down, I might be able to offer help.

He took a long swallow of his iced tea and waved to someone across the room. He apparently was paying no attention to me at all.

---I think he was making you a promise.

I pushed back from the table and draped my arm over the chair back.

---Oh?

He matched my position and put a smile on his face that could be seen on Mars.

---One of you is a dead man.

I patted my lips with my napkin and lifted my glass.

---Who you put your money on?

His eyes panned the room and he sent a wave across the tables.

---Oh, I only bet on a sure thing.

I picked up my knife and stabbed it into my steak, deliberately sawing off a chunk.

---You can book that bet.

For just a second, his hand fell on mine in benediction.

---I know.

We didn't talk any more. He was busy chewing and I was busy thinking. When the next wave of politicians surrounded the table, I nodded to my uncle and got up. He cocked a warning eye at me as he was greeting some sorry old pol, and I left.

I might not be able to prove Duplantis had anything to do with Bubber or my father. Maybe they were just incidental to one of his projects. That was of lesser importance now. That he was corrupt was one thing. That he had so little regard for anything but himself was for Divine Providence to deal with. That he had taken the most beautiful thing I had ever seen and covered her in slime was something I was going to address.

CHAPTER TWENTY-FIVE

You know, bikinis are nice, but cutoffs and a shirt tied just above the navel show about as much as a man can stand this side of a coronary. Bryna was reaching for something overhead, so I was able to examine the line of her back, swooping from her shoulders to her pertly rounded bottom.

She found the bread crusts she was reaching for, then sat beside the goldfish pond. As she tossed crusts to the fish, her shirt gaped open. Everywhere, there were the traces of wounds I wouldn't know were wounds, if I hadn't seen them when they were fresh. If the patent was available on Jimmy's salve, he should file for it because, aside from a little redness that could have been insect bites, it was hard to see the hell she'd been through. In fact, she looked damn good.

---Hello.

I held my breath, afraid to say more. Her head turned very slowly.

---Jeff.

There was no reason to tell Bryna what I knew or suspected. I couldn't tell her what I planned to do because, whatever I did, was going to take away her meal ticket. I needed to prepare her for that. I had considered several scenarios. None of them sounded good.

She studied me while I fished for words.

---You've found what you came back to find, haven't you?

She pressed her lips together until they were a thin white line and half closed her eyes like someone waiting for a punch to land. Well. It had to come out.

I could tell she knew the name before I said it. I really don't think she knew from the beginning, but I think she had begun to suspect.

---It's a judge named Duplantis.

That she was a good actress I knew. That she had nerves of steel I suspected. That she had a high tolerance for pain had been proven. What I didn't know until that moment was how much she loved me.

She didn't show fear or anger or any kind of "me" emotion. She showed hurt and it was for me. Even though she had nothing to do with anything, the fact that Duplantis had been in her bed made her feel complicit.

I was glad. she wasn't defeated, though. It wouldn't change what I was going to do, but at least she wasn't broken.

Bryna stretched out a hand to trace my jaw line. Her touch felt good and incredibly sad. Her eyes had a dangerous shine.

I threw a pebble in the pond and the fish ignored it. I guess they know food when they see it.

She sat with her hand on my knee. I could smell her clean scent and feel her warmth. All I wanted was take her in my arms. I wanted to love away everything that had happened and everything I knew, but it wasn't possible.

---Could you walk away if I asked you to?

I waited. If it came from her, it would allow her take ownership of the past. If there was going to be any "us" at any point in time, it couldn't be built on anything except the truth. Here's a news flash for you. Sometimes truth hurts.

---Why?

Her face got a very lost look and she dropped her eyes.

---I sleep with him.

I wanted to sort circuit her need to say what I already knew, so I tipped her face up to pay her the courtesy of looking in her eyes.

--- I know.

Her head turned away violently. Poor word choice. Not the most tactful thing to say, I suppose, but there was a scene to play.

---I came by one night. That gunboat was outside. He was inside.

---You spied on me?

She looked at me with a frightened face. I remembered how frail she looked when I found her.

---You heard...

I was usually better than that but my feelings were involved.

---I didn't want to...hear... I left.

One hand waved vaguely around, taking in the patio, the apartment, that said what she couldn't about the life she had been living.

---He... "keeps" me... pays for all this...

I saw her knuckles whiten as she clasped her hands as if she wanted to break something. Her jaw line hardened and she forced out the words.

---...since he does...he comes by...

Bryna twisted her hands in her lap. They must have been fascinating to watch, because she kept her focus on them.

---...and I...

Her head was down, but that inner core I admired so much brought her head up to face me and her truth.

---He screws me.

Boy, those acting classes were paying off because I kept it together. I did it for her. What she was trying to tell me wasn't the sort of thing you want people to know, especially if you want their esteem, and maybe love. I also did it for me, because it would kill me to see in her eyes that I knew what she had endured.

---He found out about you. About us. That you .... And that we...and he found out...

It wasn't the time for professions, so her head dropped and I couldn't see those amazing golden eyes.

---...how I feel about you...

Her hands clasped again and the blood left them.

---And what I ...hope you might...feel... for me...

I wanted to take her in my arms more than I wanted to take my next breath, but to do that would be to deprive her of the dignity that comes with facing your darkness.

---I don't know how he found out. He has...spies...He was very...

I knew how *very* he was. I had seen his dialogue printed on her body. She didn't know that, so she searched for a neutral word.

---He... he wanted to... teach me...

My throat closed up. My silence was weighing on us. No one I cared for so much had ever been treated as badly. I couldn't speak.

Then she said words that were beyond price.

---I'd do it all again. You and me. No matter what...Because... I...but...

She ran out of the incredible energy that had been able to sustain her.

---I... do what I have to do.

I was losing my grip on my feelings which doesn't happen often. I didn't mean the next thing to be as bitter as it came out. I didn't mean it to be as stupid as it sounded. I wished I could recall my words as soon as I spoke them.

---Well, it's a nice apartment.

Her eyes snapped to mine and her face was white.

---You son-of-a-bitch, you think I sell ass for a goddam apartment?

Having shrunk to a size smaller than Tom Thumb, I kept my mouth shut. Her shoulders slumped. There was defeat in her voice and pain in her eyes and I learned what I should have figured out, and what Don knew.

---My brother's in jail.

She got incredibly still as the life force drained away to leave behind a beautiful husk.

---I tried everything to get him out.

I didn't know if she was in pain or just relieved to finally get it all out.

---And then one day a man said he would help.

She was almost placid or maybe numb.

---If I was nice to him.

And, finally, I got what I should have been able to figure out.

---That's why you're not in One.

When she looked away, I knew I was right. The low paying job, the apartment, the "gifts" were part of an elaborate chain to bind her. And always ahead was the "favor."

She was still in the fantasy she had constructed to rationalize what she did. She'd made some very poor choices. Still, she was the person I had come to love.

I remembered the night Jimmy tended her. "The only thing left is 'snuff.'" Duplantis couldn't grant the favor or she would have no reason to continue as his toy.

---Duplantis is going to get him out.

She had to justify it, if only to herself. There was something pathetic in her certainty. She had become so precious to me. I wanted to hit someone.

---You really think people like that keep their word?

The truth was on her face, but she refused to surrender hope.

---I've... I've got to believe it.

I'd never seen her really cry. I'd seen tears in her eyes, but I never heard her sob. She was. Whatever was tearing at her was the thing that hurt her most.

--- I'm so sorry you know about me...

She brought my hand to her cheek, keeping her eyes averted.

---I wish I'd met you ...before...

I held her as tight as I could because I knew it could be for the last time.

---My brother won't last in prison. We only have each other. He's all I have...I...have to...

---Stop seeing him.

She became adamant. I saw the steel in her resolution, even as there was an ocean of regret.

---I can't...

Her dead tone froze me, and I knew. Knowledge is not always welcome when it comes. I reached for the hem of her shirt and pulled it up. She turned her head away because she knew I would find the fresh bruise.

It was hard to believe she would re-enter Hell. Not even for the mythical release of her brother from jail.

---Forget the favor. It's not going to happen. He's hurt too many people...

She pulled back, her face set in planes. It's hard to let go of a bad move, especially if you know it's a bad move.

---You understand family.

You ever see someone do something they didn't want to do but did it anyway? I have. I saw it again and it broke my heart.

I'm pretty good at reading expressions. I saw a little girl in a struggle that grew into a terrible resolve.

---Jeff...

With a tremulous smile, she unbuttoned her top and shrugged it off her shoulders, becoming a sun-lit sister to the blue vision I had seen backstage. Her cheekbones and breasts gilded, topaz eyes gushing teardrops that traced pearl rivulets down her chest.

---You don't have to go.

Stepping back, she undid the buttons of her cut offs to reveal a shining, alabaster sculpture adorned with golden accents. Hills and hollows brilliant in sunlight, she gleamed, as she had when I saw her washing off paint in the dressing room.

---...We can...

Sometimes, strength comes when you have no strength. I brought her hands to her sides and drew away, turning to the gate. There are things you don't do... abusing love is one of them. For now, at least, we had no future.

It was as hard a thing as I ever had to do, but I did it for both of us. Bryna needed to be treated with respect and I had to honor her ...personhood...People are not trash, and if you treat them as if they are, you are worse than trash.

---Stay...Please...

If I've learned anything in my life, and I'm not always sure I have, I've learned two things. First, it doesn't hurt to give a white lie about stuff if you have to. Second, always tell people you love them when you do, because you may not get that many chances, and telling someone you love them, is just about the most important information you will ever convey. I bought my hand to her, cupping her cheek. It wasn't going to change what I was going to do, and it didn't make it any easier.

---As far as I'm concerned, none of this happened...

She cried some more, stopped, turned to me and started to cry again.

---I don't know if you mean that.

---Book it, I said.

Shattered topaz eyes lowered. I wanted the chance to heal her. But if there was to be healing, it had to begin with my walking away. My heart and my head told me it was the right thing to do. My body said I was a jackass all the way to the gate.

---Jeff...

I stopped with my hand on the knob. She'd slipped her shirt on, holding it closed.

---I shouldn't have offered...

Her face was a shifting mosaic of emotions, and I saw how hard it was for her to offer her body as she had and how my rejection had made her feel even worse. I understood. Bryna was a lost little girl who'd never been loved, but who wanted to be loved, so badly.

I wanted to kiss away her tears and comb my fingers through her shining blonde hair. I wanted to hold her like the fragile prize she was.

It took a short moment and a long breath before I could answer.

--- I couldn't...You mean too much ...

---What's so special about me?

The answer to that would fill an encyclopedia, but it had to wait. Maybe, one day, I'd be able to tell her. Damn, I wanted that day to come.

CHAPTER TWENTY-SIX

Deep down, I want to believe all that stuff they told us in Civics class. My whole life had been a flight from reality, so I ended up doing plays in the Midwest at a theatre so small we had to get into our costumes in the bar next door. I didn't mind. I wasn't doing it for money. It was probably the whole escape thing. Then my dad died, and reality asked me to dance.

Nothing is easy in the Big Easy. When we get knocked down, we jump up again like pop-up dolls and say "Who dat?" (I'll explain that later.). Space had lost the use of his legs, but he had a full life. Carlo had his music. Ramirez had his work. Unc had what I can only describe as a vocation. Paul Bunyan had the fact that he kept his part of the world humming. Jimmy had medicine. Skinny had his pool hall. Don had his theatre. Me? I had a duty that I hadn't known how to fulfill.

That may be why I fell so suddenly and completely in love with Bryna. She became my life raft, offering a way in the world. Then someone pulled the plug and the air went out and I was drowning again.

So, I was at the precinct house where Ramirez was supposed to clarify the circumstances of my father's death because he was honest, dedicated and, above all, recommended by my uncle. I had been to the precinct house so many times I should have my own coffee mug on the rack. Ramirez's office felt almost homey. He didn't look homey. He looked upset. That was OK. I was too.

All my eggs were in his basket, but, instead of sunny side up, it looked like an omelet.

In my gut, I knew Duplantis was involved. I wanted him to pay for a lot of things. Most of all I wanted him to answer for Bryna.

Ramirez stopped talking. His description of what was happening on my father's case was running down, which was OK, because I had stopped listening. The short answer was, "nuttin". My dad "fell" from an overpass. At midnight. Does your dad hike an overpass at midnight? Thought not. There was nothing to indicate foul play except for a missing chunk of concrete that may not be from that night. His car was found out of gas at the foot of the ramp. Officially, he was going for gas and fell. Without a gas can.

It seemed more likely it was a chase. He was fit and he didn't shy from a fight. He just would have sought more favorable terrain.

---So, we don't have anything.

---It looks like it was accidental, but that doesn't mean he wasn't helped. But. Since we talked...

He held up his hand in the shape of a zero.

---Nothing to tie it to Duplantis?

Both hands formed double zeroes and he shrugged.

---He gets away with it?

There were wadded up paper balls on his desk and he shot them one by one across the room to a waste bin serving as a basket.

---He's skirted right on the razor's edge of the law, but he hasn't tipped over. I think your dad was in a chase that led to his fall, but there are no witnesses and no forensics.

---He fell. That doesn't mean somebody wasn't chasing him in a bigass black car so that the fall was inevitable.

---No witnesses. No proof. Logic and speculation don't go far in a court.

---Bubber?

---Well, your dad was right. It was a substandard heating system that caused his death. Our judicial friend owned the property and is responsible for the upkeep, but Bubber could easily be negligent in operating the gas heater.

He was getting better at shooting baskets but Walter Campbell wouldn't want to claim him as his own.

The next was harder but it had to be brought up. There had already been a very much off the record meet with Ramirez and Doctor Jimmy and Don at the theatre. At first Ramirez was gung-ho, but after he started digging, his ardor cooled. I needed to know why.

---Bryna?

He got very interested in balling up more paper. I suppose he was getting ready for March Madness.

He took a bottle of bourbon from his desk drawer. I hate bourbon. I didn't drink. No problem was worth drinking over. I swished some around my mouth to kill the taste of the conversation. Ramirez took a long pull.

--- There are certain... indications. He goes to her apartment. The lights are out in the bedroom window.

---Yeah. I know...

Been there. Didn't do a thing about it. Until the day I walked into the patio to learn just how he got his kicks.

---She could press charges.

---There are 'gifts' that look a lot like 'payment for services rendered.'

Bryna would never have taken money from Duplantis as a quid pro quo. But it had been made to look like the world's oldest vocation. He was keeping her and she was paying her way with very old coin. The slimy bastard set things up to provide his sorry ass cover because, if there was one thing I was sure of, it was that Bryna didn't have a "For Rent" sign around her neck.

I turned away to look at the children playing on the dirt playground while their mamas sat talking on benches under the trees. Down the white concrete steps of the red brick library, a stream of children carried books, giggling and laughing on their way to read nice stories about princesses and towers and the prince who rescues them from the ugly ogre.

---So the big, bad, black car takes the big, bad, black-robed wolf to the nearest kindergarten to show the next little girl what big teeth he has.

He slammed down his glass. Bourbon sloshed over the edge and ran across the desk to a pile of papers. He snatched them up so he wouldn't have to retype them. Two finger typing is a bitch.

---Don't go trying to be the whole judicial, legal, and penal system all by yourself.

---Never liked to star. Happier as part of an ensemble.

---No lynch mob either.

---'Course not.

I swished some more bourbon, and maybe let a little trickle down my throat. I needed to wrap this up.

---So, there's nothing I can do?

A force of nature walked into the precinct house and evening shadows suddenly fell. Everyone backed away, leaving a clear view of me through the glass wall of Ramirez's office. The huge figure saw me, smiled that smile that showed all the teeth, and waved through the glass. A happy voice rumbled through the squad room.

---Hey, Little Hammer, you still ain't done talking to the po-lice?

A rustle of relieved laughter ran through the room. The huge black figure was obviously harmless. That would have been a good assumption, unless you knew that his real smile was reserved, the bared teeth were a hunting wolf's, and the last time I heard that happy voice was just before he emptied a bar by throwing the offending parties out the window.

People went about their business. Ramirez had not moved, and his eyes never left Paul's eyes. Paul nodded his head politely, but leaned against the wall

---This is my friend Paul Bunyan.

Ramirez's face never changed, but his eyes asked the question. Paul's easy voice turned down the heat.

---Not my real name, of course. What you might call an honorific.

The smile made an appearance in Ramirez's eyes.

---I hope a large blue ox is not denuding the lawn.

---Can't afford an ox. Keep an alligator.

Ramirez laughed out loud and pulled out a chair for him. Paul put out a hand and we got down to business. His face at its most sardonic, he spread his hands wide.

---If he was caught in the act of doing something illegal.

I thought he was joking, but Ramirez didn't joke. They take points off your pension if you do. They talked. Ramirez was saying the same things, but there were overtones. I wasn't sure what it meant, but I didn't need to know. They knew.

---That warehouse in the middle of all those vacant lots.

Yeah. A neighborhood that had once been homes for people to raise families and grow old. Their kids had kids and the place was home to a lot of people. Parents and grandparents had sunk the blood and sweat of their living into the ground. Now it was a wasteland waiting for the developers.

---A couple of big policies have been written on it lately.

It wasn't the first time I'd heard about fires involving Duplantis properties.

---Anything else?

---Some of the more expensive pieces of furniture and equipment have been moved out lately.

I gave a bark of a laugh. BroBoo had told me that old tick long ago.

---Maybe somebody should take a look inside. Just to be sure all precautions have been taken.

Ramirez couldn't be around anything that smacked of illegality. He had that pension to consider.

---A good citizen might do that...

That meant me. Paul Bunyan could walk into the place and not be noticed. In a total eclipse. At midnight. On December 21st.

That left me. I'd even had some training back in the day when I entertained notions of saving democracy through service in a private "Security Company" that took on jobs the government couldn't be associated with.

When I left Ramirez, I called Charley and set up a meet at Space's place. He said he'd get BroBoo as well. All we needed was Unc, but that wasn't about to happen, politics being what it is.

In terms of approach, there was a legal path and there was another path. The legal one left us little to do. The other path meant that nobody would ever know just what it was we did which was, of course, nothing. We were home shooting pool.

Now, what was said was of importance only to the people sitting there. Since it's nobody else's business, I'm not going to say much about it. Let's just say contingencies were discussed.

Arrangements were made to meet at the warehouse. Just to reconnoiter. We'd see who was around and what was going on and what might develop. If action became necessary, we could deal with it. Or call the police. That last part was left a little vague.

CHAPTER TWENTY-SEVEN

The house I grew up in had not changed and neither had my mother. She wasn't the most demonstrative of women. I suppose I'm like her in that. She learned early in life to keep her emotions under wraps for reasons that she knew and I knew and are nobody else's business so I'm not going to talk about them here. You become a victim or you soldier on. Everybody needs a coping mechanism. I found mine on the stage. My mother was never on the stage.

The one person my mother ever opened up to was my father. Now she only had her other art form left. Drinking tea. My mother could get more out of a cup of tea than a violinist could get out of a Stradivarius. The thing was, she was the John Cage of drama queens. Spare notes and never an extraneous move.

I sat at her kitchen table drinking tea most of my adult life. Her tea ceremony was conducted with the sparseness of Zen. I inhaled the aroma of the tea and wet my lips with tiny sips. Partly because the tea was good and mostly because it was scalding hot.

The blue parakeet chirped in its cage. The copper clock shaped like a tea kettle ticked on the wall. I slurped in tiny sips.

---You been to see Space?

I sipped and nodded. She nodded.

----You been to see your uncle?

In the interest of variety, I nodded and sipped. She nodded.

----You been to see your doctor friend?

Sip. Nod. Return nod.

----You been to see that longshoreman?

For the sake of tradition, I sipped and nodded. She nodded.

----You been to see the police?

I was getting confused on sipping and nodding so I just shrugged. She nodded.

----You been to the firehouse?

I entered my special place and pulled the covers over my head. In my special place, I couldn't see her sip and nod but I know she did.

The sequel began with the accelerated chirping of the parakeet and ticking of the tea kettle clock and louder sipping and slurping from me. I'd always tried to get my mother to go faster but she never did.

---You know who it is?

---Sort of.

---You know what to do?

---I can't do anything in court and I can't tie it to dad.

---This man. He's done bad things?

---Yes.

We went silent for a while with the tea and the bird and the clock.

---I haven't been the best mother.

That was a variation I had never heard before. It was true, but which of us has ever been the best whatever?

---No complaints.

Her eyes passed through the arch leading into the kitchen to fasten on a portrait of my father. It wasn't a very good portrait, drawn not from life, but from a photograph. One of my brothers did it for a high school art assignment.

I watched her face as it became that of a young girl, a bride, a wife, and a mother. And, finally, I saw her widowhood. I saw something none of us had ever seen in her. Vulnerability passed over her face, then was replaced by the stoic mask that had enabled her to face the transient joys and permanent sorrows of life. She looked at me.

---You all had each other. All I ever wanted was him.

I reached for her hand. She let me hold it a second, then withdrew it to pick up her teacup.

---I heard about your girl. Maybe you'll finally settle down.

That didn't surprise me. She heard everything. She knew even those things we thought no one would ever know. She didn't run around town asking people questions, and getting jumped in the street, and finding, and probably losing, someone you always wanted without ever knowing you wanted her. She knew everything there was to know, sitting there drinking tea.

---Don't be soft. You were always too soft.

The phone rang and she listened for a moment before she handed it to me. Don sounded rattled. Don never sounded rattled even when he was rattled. He started right in.

---Bryna didn't come to work.

---Medical leave, remember?

---She's not at her apartment.

---Maybe she went to the "vegger-rester-bester," or whatever it's called, eating place.

Don had enough, because he cut in with the tone he used when an actor made a really stupid choice. Not that he'd ever used it with me. Much.

--- Her neighbor said she left in a big black car.

That made my stomach lurch. Why couldn't she see? Then Don's buzz saw voice got my attention.

---The neighbor thought she might be sick because two men were helping her into the car.

My attention was fully engaged. I knew what Don was thinking, because I was thinking the same. The judge was going to tie up loose ends and give a final what-for to me.

I remembered the warehouse that sat like a canker sore in what had been a neighborhood. If Duplantis was going to take her anywhere, that would be the place.

---I know where to go.

There was silence on the other end. I heard him breathing. I also thought I could hear his teeth grinding, but I could leave when it was over, whatever "it" turned out to be. He was going to stay. He rang off with his benediction.

---You better not screw this up.

When I got a dial tone I made a call to my cop shop. He answered on the first ring, so I figured he was waiting.

---I was thinking of taking a ride this afternoon. Any ideas about a good place for a drive?

There was a pause and I could hear his fingers drumming on his desk as he did the mental arithmetic about the years to his pension.

---Try the warehouse district. I hear there's activity there.

Ramirez all but told me he had the warehouse staked out.

---Will I see you there?

I could see his hand grip the phone and hear him chew his lip.

---I only go after criminals.

---Well, if I see one I'll give you a call.

He grunted and I started to hang up but he shot in a quick question.

---Got a ride?

---Not really.

---Cabs might be hard to find, but some people run jitneys when they're not working their regular jobs. Like on the riverfront.

OK. Either I was very bright or it was all very obvious, because I got that one, too.

---See you.

---Not right away.

He rang off and I sat there trying to decide how I was going to take my leave. Shouldn't have worried. My mother always knew everything anyhow. There was, of course, the obligatory sip of tea first.

---Go do what needs doing.

---OK.

There was the dead silence that indicated it was time for the coda.

---Will you be back for tea?

I took my cup to the sink, rinsed it out, put it in the dishwasher, and looked out the window at her garden. It was the greenest place I'd ever seen. She could grow anything. I was going to miss it, and her, and our silent communions.

---Not for a while.

Spartan mothers sent their sons off to war with more emotion. She took a long sip of her tea and wiped her glasses on the hem of her dress.

---Take care of yourself.

Paul Bunyan was waiting in the old black Plymouth my father sold him years before. I gave a silent laugh. There was no way Ramirez would ever make his pension. On the other hand, things are seldom straightforward in New Orleans, and friends were good to have. I ran my hand over the dashboard. Paul loved that car. He kept it running and would never replace it. We know about relics down here. I got in without being invited and we sat in a silence that carried over from the kitchen.

---Figured you'd be here.

There was no tea to sip but I could nod and I did.

---That warehouse? That judge done brought your lady there. I think she's bait.

---I think I'll take it.

He put the car into gear and we drove to a wasteland that was once an Eden. There were other figures in the shadows. We sat staring straight ahead.

---Ain't seen no sign of Ramirez.

---Not to worry. The boy could have been an actor. He's got a sense of timing.

---Judge's got cameras around, so you need to be careful.

That was good to know. If I got to the control room, I could use their video system to scout the warehouse so I didn't risk my neck.

Paul Bunyan's huge presence filled the car. It would be comforting to have him by my side, but he would be staying in New Orleans after I left, too.

----This isn't your fight. I'll go by myself.

A dark liquid chuckle filled the car and I felt warmer.

---Little Hammer, sometimes you talk the stupidest trash.

I slipped out the door and crossed the sidewalk quickly flattening against the wall while the car, which had never really stopped, continued down the street to park around the corner.

Other people were waiting outside, but you're not going to know who they were. I'm a great believer in plausible deniability. Of course, if you're not a moron, you already know who they were. Our group assembled silently, plastered to the wall like decals. It was unlikely a camera would pick us up.

---Can you get me in without being seen?

The night grew darker as a huge shadow covered us.

---If you want to insult me, just say ugly things about my mama.

The door was opened, a perimeter established, and I was inside. BroBoo left to scout, while Charley and I went to the video room. Paul Bunyan vanished once he bent the door off its hinges like he was playing with Silly Putty.

The security cameras covered the entire building. My fingers flew over the switches as I tried to find Bryna. My hand froze on the board as her nude image appeared on the screen. Her hands and feet were fastened to the legs of a chaise with rope that cut into her skin. A video camera on a tripod was trained on her. There was a desk, so I figured she was in his office.

I set off at a run. I had a lot to do in a hurry and I was having trouble prioritizing. It was done for me when the first charge went off with a dull whoosh. Of course, he wouldn't use big ones. It was going to be an accident, after all. That meant there would be several and I'd have some time to maneuver.

If he was setting them off with Bryna tied and helpless, I had a pretty good idea her usefulness to him was ended. He planned to see her off, and have his own personal snuff film to remember her by. Problems were multiplying around me, and I was running out of options. I sent Charley to free her and BroBoo to keep an eye on the fire to see it didn't spread to areas we were occupying. With everybody disposed, my job was to tree the fox. I knew where he would go. Before he left, he would want the tape of Bryna.

The building was fully engaged. Flames were shooting from rooms on either side. Heat rolled from the flames and into the hall. Even though I knew it was a fire with all the potential for death and destruction that a fire entails, I never thought of that. My family had too many firefighters for flames to panic me.

Duplantis was in there somewhere, and he wasn't going to get away. The thought that something bad might happen to me never entered my mind. I doubt it was courage. It was stupidity. Or a failure of imagination. At any rate, as I went further into the building, I tripped over a shapeless lump that turned out to be

Charley. Musicians are as useless as actors in a crisis. BroBoo was coming down the hall.

---Never send a musician to do a firefighter's job.

—- Get Charley out. I'll get Bryna.

I felt my way down the hall, keeping my face a foot above the floor as my father taught me. You don't want to lie flat in a fire. The toxic gasses hug the floor and they kill you. A foot above, there is still oxygen.

Checking for landmarks I noted on the cameras, I found the office. The chaise was in the center of the room with Bryna still tied to it. She saw me and her eyes filled.

---I asked him not to hurt you. He said he wouldn't. Then two men came for me.

No time to talk, I worked on the knots.

---I'm sorry. I'm so sorry.

Yeah, I was, too. After I untied her, I threw my coat over her. Pointing to the door, I said one word.

---Out.

She nodded and I crawled across the office to the other door. I heard Duplantis call from somewhere to my left.

---Actor? I know you're here. I had eyes on you since you got to town. It got personal when you decided to plow my field.

All those edgy feelings I tried to put down to imagination had been real. I always said, "it wasn't paranoia if they really were out to " blah blah blah.

---Thought I was out of town, but I had eyes on her. I never leave my property unattended.

---She's not property.

---You wrong there. Her ass is bought and paid for. She was worth it, until she decided to do you.

I'd thought I'd felt tails on me, but that'd sounded crazy even to me, though the fact that I was right didn't surprise me. As for Duplantis, I'd already decided he was playing with forty-eight cards, at best. He gave the same satyr's laugh I'd heard at Ruth's.

---I can tell you when you did her and how many times. 'Sall right. I had her ways you never even thought of.

He'd had Bryna's place rigged with cameras so he could get off by watching what he had her do. It became surveillance when I entered her life.

--- I ain't Huey Long. I don't share nothing.

He had it planned. Bryna would die in the fire. Her brother would die in jail. He'd have his tapes, including the last one, to watch as long as they still did it for him. Then he would buy another person and play Marquis de Sade all over again. That gave me another reason to edge him toward that great green room in the sky.

--- Time for your last scene. But there won't be no bowing when it's over.

He was probably around the corner. My view was blocked by some construction debris, but I was reasonably sure it was a dead end. He sure as hell didn't intend for me to get out. But he wanted to get out. He had money and power and he wanted to enjoy them. If he ruined a few lives along the way, that was a bonus.

The fire, which had been burning cleanly, was now producing a lot of smoke that'll kill you. Of course, the building falling on you wouldn't help, but it was usually the toxic gases. I stayed my safe foot above the floor.

As I crawled to the corner, I saw a couple of shoe tips protruding from behind the debris. If all I could see was his shoe tips, he was waiting to get me when I walked around the corner. In that case, if I could get a little closer, I could come up from underneath and nail him instead. Daddy's Little Baby might end up a witness in court after all. That was a very happy thought, because I wanted him dead less than I wanted him humiliated. Well, I wanted both. But dead was too easy.

I was just my side of the corner, getting my legs under me to spring, when a voice cut through the noise of the fire.

---Chaussier !

Bryna. For an actress, she had lousy timing. She must have been crawling down the hall to escape the smoke, because her voice was low to the ground. When Duplantis heard her, he looked down. There I was.

Fortunately, he wasn't real bright, or else he was a sportsman. Instead of kicking me in the head then knocking me senseless to finish me off, he jumped on me. Since I was in the process of coming up when he did, I caught him full in the stomach with my shoulder. I heard air whoosh out of him. If I could take advantage of that, I could have him down before he regained his breath.

---Chaussier!

Damn, but she had a one-track mind. I turned my head to her voice.

---Get the hell out of here, I yelled.

There's a reason chivalry is dead. The people who practiced it got themselves killed looking after their lady instead of paying attention to the bad guys. When I turned, I gave him the split second he needed. Instead of seeing my blonde, I saw stars.

It was probably a two by four from the pile. It felt like one. I went all the way to the floor. He was no gentleman after all. He kicked me in the face, just like he always should have done.

I rolled fast to avoid another and got my feet under me. You don't want to be flat on the floor if you're going to fight a nut case in a fire. Of course, if you're in a fire and fighting, the question of which one of you is the nut case does not have an easy answer.

Instead of waiting for a shot that would finish me off, I scrabbled across the hall to the other side. The smoke was denser and he would have trouble seeing me. I kept my back to the wall and slid up as flat as I could to keep the target small. He mimicked Bryna in a falsetto.

---Chaussier, he called.

The man certainly knew how to do nasty laughs because I got another one.

---You're going to end up in the fire, actor. No funeral for you to star in.

I saw something that surprised me. The damn fool didn't have a gun. He had a knife. Was he very dumb or very smart? He was smart. If he got me in the fire with a knife, there'd be no forensics to prove I'd been killed. Just another unfortunate accident in an unlucky family. I didn't want that to happen. Among other reasons, there was the fact that I really did want to star in my own funeral. Actors love curtain calls.

At about that time, I heard the sound of water from a hose and the smoke got knocked down for a second. BroBoo was on the job. The smoke parted and I saw the future defendant clearly.

He didn't know how to hold a knife; he held it by the haft perpendicular to the floor. I knew better. I'd been a Jet in "West Side Story." I was very good. Forget the critics.

I thought the way he handled a knife made him an amateur, but that may be unfair. The bloody knife was the size of a small sword.

---Chaussier! Bryna called again.

Dammit.. If ever anybody ever needed a dialogue writer it was her.

Twice an idiot--once for coming into the fire after me, and twice for calling out to alert him, Bryna finally did something smart. She stood up when the smoke cleared and ran down the hall. Actually, that was also potentially stupid, because she put herself in danger. But, since she was naked, it worked out just fine.

Duplantis took a second to leer and that gave me a chance to make a move. I jumped him from behind and went straight for the knife arm.

There was an explosion and a whoosh as something ignited in the blaze. A blast of heat and a billow of smoke filled the hall as I landed on him. I couldn't see Bryna, but I wasn't looking. I had all I could handle with him. He seemed determined not to "go gentle into that good night" and I wasn't going anywhere, so we had a pretty good tussle.

We got to our feet, our weight shifting back and forth, each looking for an advantage. I had forgotten too much of my old training, and he was too out of shape for it to be an interesting fight, so it doesn't bear a lot of narration.

I was either better motivated or meaner, because I got the advantage on him and the knife was moving away from my guts. He could see he was losing.

---You think you gonna put me on trial? You been in too many plays.

For just that second, I felt ice in my gut. There was more than a fair chance he was right. I'm as patriotic as the next guy and I believe in the rule of law, but I had seen its practice up close and personal too often to be idealistic about it. That left me with an ethical dilemma on my hands and his knife too near my gut for comfort.

---Little Hammer? a deep voice called out in the gloom.

—-He's here, Bryna called in the gloom.

I turned to look. Bad move.

Duplantis made a quick lunge and I felt the trickle on my stomach that told me I had been nicked. I made the amateur's mistake of looking to see how badly I was cut. The end result was that the knife whipped around and headed toward me. I winced and shut my eyes, which was also stupid, but not many of us want to look at their own death when they see it approaching.

There wasn't a harp to be heard so I slowly opened my eyes. An arm the size of a tree trunk was around the judge's neck and, from the color of the judge's face, the arm was squeezing tightly. Paul got his legs under him. I knew the position. He was gathering the force to shove upward. When he did, the knife would plow into Duplantis, slicing his abdomen open.

The bad part was that the smoke cleared one final time and Bryna saw the tableau clearly. Me, Paul, and a knife near the judge's gut.

She screamed.

---Don't kill him!

For the final Wagnerian touch, there was another explosion which sent smoke and fire into the hall.

Bryna cut the Gordian knot by yelling my name again. There were too damn many people calling my name in the middle of a knife fight. I lunged toward her as she ran down the hall, putting a hand across her eyes. Squinting against the smoke and heat, I saw a brief tussle then action froze.

A hand came out of nowhere to fasten on Paul's wrist. I couldn't see the guy's face, but his head shook from side to side.

Now, nobody could keep Paul from doing anything he wanted, but Paul seemed to know this guy. When the guy shook his head, Paul stepped to the side.

There were two men, neither of whom I would care to meet in a dark alley. Even with Paul and an armored cavalry division for backup. Having done Greek tragedy, I recognized that Olympus was intervening.

----He's not for you.

His partner put a friendly hand on Paul's shoulder.

---This is a business matter.

It was New Orleans, a Mediterranean city that understood men like these, even if the root they grew from was a long way from the Mississippi.

Anyway, the first one moved into position. The second pulled Duplantis' head back. I think they wanted him to see what was coming. They said something I couldn't hear and Duplantis' eyes got wide. The guy with the choke hold nodded to the guy with the knife who struck, driving the blade in deep.

There was a scream. Damn. I forgot Bryna. I made a quick dive and caught her just before she hit the floor.

Duplantis made a gurgling sound and turned his head to me. His eyes told me I was to blame, but that wasn't so. He'd brought it on himself. We mostly do.

No one would ever know who his executioners were. Do you? Certainly not me. Sometimes it's just nice to be around when The Kindly Ones make their appearance.

Scooping Bryna into my arms, I rolled onto my back with her on top of me and my handkerchief over her nose.

I looked back in time to see Nemesis throw the judge's body into the fire and the knife into a bucket of cement. They disappeared into the smoke, because they were never there. Paul had gone, too, because he was never there either. Would you say he was?

I found the coat Bryna dropped and stuck her arms through the sleeves. Too many people were seeing more of her than you see of a Bourbon Street stripper on a Saturday night. Keeping as close to the floor as I could while avoiding that deadly foot of gases, I used my legs to scoot us down the hall to the stairwell. Luckily, Charley and BroBoo were climbing them.

Outside, Ramirez was waiting at the door with a squad car. He bundled me and Bryna inside and tapped on the hood. A cop I'd never seen, who wasn't there anyway, drove us off in a car I never sat in. Ramirez turned to a slew of arriving cars to play at keeping the city safe. Only, Ramirez didn't play.

I tugged the coat over Bryna and buttoned it all the way up so the driver could stop looking in the rear-view mirror.

You gotta love those fade outs in the movies where the boy and girl disappear into a sunrise that forecasts light and love and a rosy future. Well, I was pretty certain that, like the song says, "They're writing songs of love, but not for me."

Not just then.

CHAPTER TWENTY-EIGHT

I went by the theatre to tell Don I was leaving. He saw my face as I climbed the stairs to his office and picked up a bottle. I shook my head.

---No scotch?

---Not a good idea right now.

He was right. It never had been for me. He poured two cups of coffee.

I'd been doing stuff that had to be done, then I was leaving. Unc had been Delphic at City Hall. Though I was sure he knew, he said nothing about the Deliverers who showed up at the warehouse. He didn't need to.

If you know how the body works to promote health, you know the white blood cells are as important as the red. You won't find it in the Civics books or law courts, but I think you can find it in the Bible.

I'd seen Paul. It hadn't been Paul's hand that drove the knife home, but it wouldn't have been his first time. Before he worked the docks, he'd done some Army time in a unit that doesn't exist doing things that do not happen. He'd tired of it and retreated to his little part of New Orleans where his presence kept the peace and his formidable strength enforced it.

Paul was the towering *paterfamilias* and Ramirez was Joshua, doing the work while striving toward the promised land of his thirty. Ramirez had no idea how his men happened to show up. There just happened to be six squad cars and two fire companies in the area at the time. As to my dark avengers, his face was as bland as the "who?" he responded with. There was more to Ramirez than I knew and I suspected Unc's fine hand could be found somewhere in the works. That's why I could leave. Things were going to be as they should.

I'd said my good- byes to my family. Well, that's not true. With people you love, it's always, "see ya." I knew that was true of them and Don. I wasn't sure about Bryna, which was why I was sitting with a cup of toxic black brew in my hands.

Don and I engaged in our cryptic communion that consisted of things not said and words a half notch off true north. He knew what was on my mind, but he would never bring it up. No one understood our communication, because no one understood our connection. I'm not sure we did.

Bryna's name never came up. He wouldn't and I couldn't. It would be resolved, in time; meantime she would be in the fold. That would have to do. He walked me down the stairs to the lobby, but I couldn't make myself step across the doorsill separating the theatre from the world.

He saw me hesitating and nodded his head toward backstage but I shook my head. I hate painful good-byes. I gave him a final abrazo and started for the door to the street. I have no idea how I ended up in the dressing room. My sense of direction was always lousy. Who was I kidding? Not Don. Not even me. The truth was I had something more to do. So, I saw Bryna one last time before I left.

I knew she wasn't going to be happy. She had to find a new apartment. She had to sort out what she had done and why. Don would help. Ramirez and Jimmy would help. My uncle would help. I couldn't. For right now, at least, I was part of the problem.

I was the guy who canceled her meal ticket and kept the key turned on her brother. That I might also have saved her life and maybe, her sanity, she couldn't process just yet. I hoped she would work it out. If she did, Don would let me know and I would be back. Old Monte Cristo was right. Wait and hope.

She had healed up nicely. If you looked closely, you could still see some of the marks, but you had to know where to look, and you had to look carefully. I was able to do both because she was mother naked. One of the few blessings of the theatre is that women are always changing costume and, should the gods smile, you get to see them in their birthday suits. I, of course, am too much of a gentleman to look. That I always looked at Bryna was indicative of the fact that I felt we could be one flesh until death. Or I was a pervert.

She always had radar about me, because she seemed to know I was there. Our eyes met in the mirror and she reached for her robe. The one good thing was that she did a 360. I'd like to think she did it for me, to let me see her one last time. I could be wrong. Her mood wasn't loving. Angry eyes, more like burnished bronze than gold, cut through me like an Assyrian sword.

---You had to kill him?

---I didn't.

---Then you hired those men to do it.

For right now, it was easier to focus her anger on me. To her, I was the reason Duplantis had a job making license plates for Satan. There was no time to go into the why of it. He had killed himself, though she wouldn't have understood how and the knowledge was potentially dangerous anyway. I took a simpler path that still hinted at the truth.

---I believe it was ruled an accidental death in a fire.

She didn't buy it. I wouldn't have either.

---What's going to happen to my brother?

---I have an uncle who is not without influence, and that's an understatement, in case you were wondering.

Her eyes were trying to see what I was getting at.

---And I have a policeman friend. They've promised to look into the case.

---Will they get him out?

---They can get his time shortened. If he behaves himself.

Her face froze and her body stiffened as she told again a lie she had forced herself to believe.

---Duplantis was going to get him out.

It was painful to see how doggedly she clung to that fiction. I understood it had been her justification for so long it had become a part of her. Dr. Jimmy had a friend at the hospital who had offered free counseling and Don had promised to see that she went. Don could be very persuasive. Just then, she was too deep in illusion.

---Duplantis was going to get him out. That's why I ... I would never have ... I'm not a...

Her eyes dropped. I was glad she didn't finish. I didn't want to know what she had done because of Duplantis' promise and I don't believe she really wanted to tell me. She gave up trying to explain the inexplicable and shrugged.

---He promised.

Theirs had been a sick nexus that had to end. I would have preferred someone else ended it. I felt little guilt for what happened to Duplantis, but it hadn't helped Bryna.

After a moment, her shoulders gave a slight shrug and she raised her eyes to me.

---He promised.

There are things it takes a long time to face, and longer to admit, and still longer to deal with. I can testify to that. I was going to have to go through my own process. I had sacrificed her chance at what she so desperately wanted on the altar of my duty. I could admit that, but I wouldn't beat myself up about it. To avoid dealing with it, I got mad with the anger of one who knows an unpalatable truth.

---Duplantis was going to ride your ass like a hobby horse while your brother rotted in jail, then leave you under a streetlight on Chartres Street with fishnet stockings and a cigarette dangling from the corner of your mouth.

I almost got her to laugh. If she had, I would have stayed in New Orleans, but she didn't, and that told me the time just wasn't right.

--- I don't know who you are, she said.

She held her stare for a long time before she dropped her eyes, so I told her the truest thing I knew.

---Then, I guess it's good I do, I said.

I thought those were pretty accurate parting words on both sides. She didn't call me back, so I kept going.

Far in the distance, a bolt of lightning lit the sky. It took a long time for the sound of the thunder to reach me, so I knew vivifying rain was still far off.

Old Tom Lanier, the playwright not the poet, was on my mind as I left. Bryna's world was lit by lightning and she huddled in it with her illusions. I hoped she wouldn't blow the candles out and I'd be able to come back to light a new flame. Perhaps, eventually, she would process things and, maybe, forgive.

I left the theatre and walked down streets filled with drunken tourists who were going to go back to Iowa and talk about all the sin they found in New Orleans. They didn't know the half of it.

The concourse of the airport was quiet at that late hour. I picked up my ticket and sat at the gate waiting. I didn't buy a magazine. I had plenty to think about.

Usually, I was terrified of flying. That's why I had taken the bus when I returned to New Orleans. After the events of the last few weeks, crashing didn't seem like a big deal. Besides, I wanted to put as much distance between me and the Queen City of the South as I could, as soon as I could.

That didn't mean I wouldn't be back. I had family here. I had friends here. Bryna was here. The place was in my blood like the rich chocolate waters of the Mississippi and the coffee and chicory we brew from them. I couldn't stay away. But I could go away. Right now, I had to.

The plane dipped its wing as it circled the city to pass over the dark blot of Lake Pontchartrain. The lights of the city nestled in the crescent of the river's big bend past Algiers. Whenever I saw that sight, I always thought New Orleans sparkled like a bracelet on the wrist of a beautiful woman. Looking at her lights as I left, I guess she did.

But I'd learned how deceiving the image of a beautiful woman can be.

THE END

About the Author

George Sanchez, a native New Orleanian and a member of ACTORS' EQUITY, SAG-AFTRA and the DRAMATISTS GUILD. With family and pug dog, he lives in New Orleans where he writes and produces a monthly cable television program.

Previous publications include: "Uncle Earl," a play about Louisiana's colorful governor Earl Long.

Jeff Chaussier novels include Lit by Lightning, Exploration's End, A Place Unchanged, Shreds and Patches, A-Roving No More, To Wake the Sleeper, Where Are the Snows? and A Slow Trek with more coming.

He has also published a non-Jeff book set in New Orleans during November 1963, Looking For Tennessee Williams.

He has co-authored two books, Both Sides of the Curtain, a theatre textbook, with Jim Winter; and Riding the Rim, a travel book with Terry Forrete.

Praise for the Jeff Chaussier Mysteries

… descriptions of the Crescent City seem almost poetic ("New Orleans has no star. She is an ensemble piece"). --**Kirkus Reviews**

New Orleans is a vibrant, electric city that serves as the perfect backdrop in this second book in the Jeff Chaussier New Orleans Mystery series. – **SPR**

The author is at his best when depicting the food, the smells, and the buildings and docks of the French Quarter (some readers may even target the Big Easy as their next travel destination). --**Kirkus Reviews**

Likable characters being an apparent necessity in genre fiction, Sanchez, much to his credit, plays with that notion by creating a few who're amiable, sexy. And wholly deceptive. --**Indie Reader**

His humor-infused narrative flows easily and he has a real knack for using descriptions to effectively convey the slightest changes in mood and atmosphere. – **SPR**

…Sanchez creates appealing characters and vivid images, his prose elevated by a flair for the absurd: "A cigar and a Marine tattoo did not go well with a blonde wig and mascara…" --**Kirkus Reviews**

If there is truth in Theodore Roosevelt's proverbial "Nobody knows how much you know until they know how much you care," then George Sanchez's third Jeff Chaussier New Orleans Mystery might qualify as its vessel. --**Indie Reader**

With healthy dollops of charm and wit, *Exploration's End* serves up a satisfying mystery that is sure to please fans of the genre. – **SPR**

An addictive romance/adventure with well-developed protagonists. — **Kirkus Reviews**

www.ingramcontent.com/pod-product-compliance
Lightning Source LLC
Chambersburg PA
CBHW070109260626
47160CB00004B/1385